BINWELL SINYANGWE studied Industrial Economi Sciences in Bucharest, Romania, where he was awarded an M.Sc. in 1983. His first novel, *Quills of Desire*, was published by Baobab Books in Zimbabwe in 1993. It was also published in South Africa by Heinemann in 1996. The story 'Wild Coins' was published in an anthology of stories by Zambian writers. Sinyangwe has also had a number of articles and poems published in Zambian newspapers and magazines.

Binwell Sinyangwe is a widower, and lives in Lusaka with his son and two daughters.

MW00779045

BINWELL SINYANGWE

A COWRIE OF HOPE

Heinemann

Heinemann is an imprint of Pearson Education Limited, a
company incorporated in England and Wales, having its registered
office at Edinburgh Gate, Harlow, Essex, CM20 2JE.
Registered company number: 872828

www.heinemann.co.uk

Heinemann is a registered trademark of Pearson Education Limited

First published in 2000

British Library Cataloguing in Publication Data
A catalogue record for this book is available from the British Library.

Cover design by Touchpaper
Cover illustration by Voti Thebe

Phototypeset by SetSystems Ltd, Saffron Walden, Essex

Printed by Multivista Global Ltd.

ISBN 978 0 435912 02 4

20 19 18 17 16 15 14 13

IMP 16 15 14 13

To the loving memory of
My wife, Grace

Part One

*There is no hope except under
the shadow of the gods*

Chapter One

The ulcer is burning deep

The whirlwind of desperation inside her was carrying, pushing her like a blade of grass towards the unthinkable. She thought once again: Is this the way things must end? This time, unlike the others when the question had repeated itself in her head, she answered: No, I have made the decision, tomorrow morning I shall do it – I shall go to Mangano and approach Isaki.

She was perched on a stool before a fire she had kept lit between the three stones at the hearth of her hut, holding her hands out to the warmth and gazing as though spellbound at the red glow which was shimmering like an expiring heart among the stones. The May night was so dark that had it not been for the glare of the flames, it would have been impossible to see anything.

The hut sat askew, helpless on the earth like an abandoned child, alone, away from the other homes of the village. Old, and sodden with shame from dilapidation and squalor. Everything about the dwelling, from its crack-ridden floor to its sagging roof and the dearth of its contents, told a rending story of poverty.

There, in that furnace of squalor and privation, she the owner of the hut, sat hunched before the hearth, facing the horizon where the sun disappears. Her slender body was thin, her face tense and pale. Her dark tufts of hair rose crooked and unkempt. Absorbed in her thoughts, she cried in silence for help from the most unthinkable and dreaded source, Isaki the son of Chiswebe.

The woman was troubled. It was midnight, everybody in the

3

village would be fast asleep, yet sleep would not come for her. Wide awake, her dark eyes open and dry, she stared vacantly at the fire. So it was with her these days. After a hard day of endless pursuit, of searching for a solution to her problem, midnight would find her awake, thinking and worrying, asking herself the question: What shall I do? When desperation gave way to fear, the fear of her daughter's schooling coming to an end, her thoughts would stiffen and she would silently lament: Is this the way things end?

Her name, Nasula, meant mother of Sula and the meaning of Sula, her daughter's name, was 'let things be'. But Nasula, she who was supposed to be the mother of letting things be, would not let things be over her daughter's schooling. She insisted that her daughter must continue with her schooling and so she told her only daughter and the people she spoke to in search of help with her problem.

Sula her daughter's schooling. That was her worry, the beginning and ending of her problem. The child had completed grade nine at Senga Hill Basic School and had passed. She could now go on to grade ten at a distant, boarding, secondary school, St Theresa Girls in Kasama. She needed one hundred thousand *kwacha* for the child's fares, school fees and other requirements. But she, her mother and only living parent, did not have the money. She did not have any money, not even one coin, anywhere in the world.

Nasula was poverty, she was loneliness and aloneness. Suffering was her life. She wore it like her own skin. A young peasant woman in her early thirties, beautiful and gracefully built, Nasula had no means and no dependable support. She was the gods' plant growing on poor soils without tendrils. Both her parents had died not long after she had come of age and had left her with nothing but herself. Her late husband had left her some money and goods, but hardly before his funeral was over,

4

her in-laws had swooped everything out of her possession and left her to languish with nothing in her hands, alone with her only daughter and child. She had lived like that to this day, poor, parentless, widowed and without a relative to talk to and to whom she could turn.

But misfortune had not caged the woman's soul. Poverty, suffering and never having stepped into a classroom had not smoked her spirit and vision out of existence. Her humanity continued to be that which she had been born with, one replete with affection and determination. It was this which fanned her desire to fight for the welfare of her daughter. Her soul had eyes that saw far and a fire that burned deep. She understood the importance of education and wanted her daughter to go far with her schooling. She understood the unfairness of the life of a woman and craved for emancipation, freedom and independence in the life of her daughter. Emancipation, freedom and independence from men.

Nasula was poor, illiterate and clothed in suffering, but she was an enlightened woman possessed with a sense of achievement. She had not tasted success in her own life, but she wanted her daughter to achieve much. She wanted her daughter to reach mountain peaks with her schooling and from there carve a decent living that would make it possible for her not to depend on a man for her existence.

Nasula's whirlwind marriage to Winelo, the first-born of Chiswebe, a citified faker from these parts; her stay in the capital city where Winelo had shifted her (away from the traditional village fastnesses) a week after an acquaintance in the village had hurriedly married her off; and her life following the death of Winelo. These were the things whose light and darkness had opened her eyes and fired her soul. What she had seen and heard and gone through along their pathways, had awakened her to the indignities and injustices of a woman who could only put her life in the hands of a man, and to the possibility of a good education giving a woman independence and freedom.

Nasula had not forgotten. She would not forget. How could she? They had turned her into a servant, a slave in a chief's palace. They had turned her into a stream in which to wash and kill the stink of their humanity. They had turned her into the hunter's flat stone on which to sharpen their spears and axes. Into *icisongole* to play *iciyenga* with during the day, a fruit to be eaten at by the chief during the night. Into a source of laughter.

They had made her look like a non-human, a doll without thoughts or feelings of her own. Winelo and his relatives. Winelo, her late husband. Let his soul rest in peace. She had loved him, she still loved him even as he was dead. He too had loved her and, she was sure, still loved her even in death. But he had accepted and enjoyed the ways of the day and the world, to be master over her and turn her into a plaything to use and to laugh at.

Why? She was a woman. Just a woman. One without means at that. Without Winelo, where or what would she be?

'He keeps her, he feeds her, he buys her clothes . . .' they would sing to the whole world in naked daylight. 'She even looks washed, because of him. If you had seen her when he brought her from the village!'

Let her tire of it and complain to Winelo and he would turn into a true Chiswebe. He would come at her with the purring of a wild cat and the coldness of the muzzle of a loaded gun.

'Woman, don't I keep you, or maybe it's you who keeps me? Is it not me who buys the food in this house? Is it not me . . . ?'

'The way things are said . . .'

'Do you want everybody in the world to talk the way you want them to talk and avoid telling the truth?'

6

'Insulting and humiliating others, is that the right or only way of telling the truth?'

'A woman will never appreciate a thing. Look, Nasula, why don't you just pack and tell me to give you transport money so that you can go back to the village if you are tired of being in a marriage with me? I can bring in someone else this very moment.'

On two occasions, her pride had been injured beyond what she could bear. She cried, packed, and asked him for her bus fare back to the village. He had enough money on him but he said he did not have enough money to spend on journeys that were not decided upon by him.

'It is you who has decided to go, not me. Why don't you also look for money to pay for your journey?' he had said on the first occasion.

'You know I have no money.'

'Why then have you decided to go?'

'Father of Sula, help me. Let me go back where you found me. You brought me here.'

'Was that a mistake I made?'

'To bring me here to insult me for what you give me and do for me?'

'Nasula, you are too full of yourself. That's what's with you! Ata!'

'I am poor and a woman, but you do not stop being a human being when you are poor or a woman.'

'Pride will kill you, woman.'

'Pride is the only thing I own in the world. What shall become of me if I lose even my pride?'

'Unpack those things and stop behaving like a child.'

'Give me money for the bus and let me go.'

Pain had constricted her throat and she had cried like a child stolen away from its mother.

On the second occasion, she had gone further and tried to look for money. When word had leaked out to Winelo, he had accused her of being on the way to becoming flesh for the street.

She had not forgotten and she would not forget. How could she? The faces and voices of those young women of good education and good jobs in offices who came to Kalingalinga shanty compound, where she lived with Winelo, to talk to the women of the compound about the freedom of the woman. What they said about the importance of knowing how to read and write and of having a good education, what they said about the rights of a woman, and the need for a woman to stand on her own.

How they unmasked a man and reduced the devil to dust. How they cried for awareness and hailed the strength and power of a woman. Those young women. Sweet, sparkling creatures of the gods. They were freedom itself. Light and hope. In them she saw Sula her daughter and in Sula she saw them.

How could she forget what happened after the death of her husband? Chiswebe, the father of the deceased, and Isaki Chiswebe, the young brother to the deceased (Isaki was the fourth-born and oldest son of Chiswebe after Winelo) came to Lusaka, together with his relatives and others of Chiswebe's children. After the burial, the news was broken to her that Isaki Chiswebe would be taking over as her husband. She knew Isaki and his ways in things of the flesh very well. She also now knew the Chiswebe family too well to remain married to one of its members. She refused to be married to Isaki.

How they turned against her. Blamed her for the death of the husband. People of the world, how could anyone blame her for the death of a man who had been shot by policemen while he was stealing? She had not even known, until his death, that Winelo had taken to stealing. What she had known was that he

8

worked for a company that repaired vehicles and sold spare parts for different machines. She had not known that seven months before the police had found her husband and his friends hauling stolen tins of paint into a van from the yard of a company that made paint, and had shot him and two others as they had tried to run away, that he had been sacked by the company he worked for after being caught and proved to have stolen a car battery belonging to the company.

She was demanding, she had caused her husband to go and steal. So they said. Gods' people, which day? Nasula, the poorest woman under the sun, she who was grateful even for a cup of water so dirty as to be mud, of all things, to haunt a man into stealing such big things as Winelo had met his death stealing? What falsehood! Had the gods and spirits no eyes to see? Were the lies not an excuse for hidden intentions?

When he was about to die – Winelo knew that he was dying and should think of the wife and child he was leaving behind – he told the policeman who was guarding him in the hospital to give him a pen and a clean sheet of paper. On the paper the policeman fetched for him from a doctor in the ward, he wrote that for the sake of his child, Sula Chiswebe, his house in Kalingalinga and everything in it that he was leaving behind, including the money to the sum of seven hundred and fifty thousand *kwacha*, should be given to his wife, Nasula, and that his parents and relatives should share only his gun, his bicycle and his clothes.

What was the use? Was the man who was given to read the words the deceased had written even allowed to finish reading? How they frowned upon everything and tore the paper on which the words were written to pieces. How they took away everything from her except what was on her body. How they threw her out of the house and sold it, leaving her to spend nights at

9

the bus station with the child before she found money for her travel and returned to the village.

What of the child? Who could be sure that it was Winelo's blood, they said. Had Winelo not been overheard telling her that she was flesh for the street?

No, she would not forget. The way she was suffering after Winelo her husband had died. The way she was suffering back here in the village after the man, Winelo, had taken her to the city and made her used to a modern life where he gave her what material things she needed, only to die a careless death and condemn her back to rags and sand because she was incapable of acquiring such things on her own. This was the price she was paying for having placed her whole life in the hands of a man, for having forgotten to hold her destiny in her own hands, even as she had been married.

Her thoughts suddenly became too painful. She tried to put them behind her. The fire before and below her outstretched hands disappeared. A darkness covered her and the image of Winelo filled her mind: strongly built, dark-skinned, flat-nosed, large horn-like ears and sharp, inquisitive eyes. A human being who surely could not have stolen or told a lie or belittled a wife and boasted about what he gave her and did for her.

She stared long at him. He became alive and real, she could smell and feel him. Her emotions rose higher and higher. She wept and whispered silently: Help me, father of Sula. The child must go to school. Help me with the money for her school or I shall die of this pain. The ulcer of my poverty is burning deep.

A noise of the rising of a soul came from behind her. She returned to the world. The unearthly darkness that had covered her vanished. The image of Winelo went with it. The darkness of the night, the smell of the earth, the cracked wall and sooty roof of the hut, and the smouldering fire in the hearth returned and restored her overwrought senses. She turned in the direction

10

of the noise and saw the only other inhabitant in the lonely hut rising from her lying position, the soul at the heart of her worries, the soul that was her life and death. Sula, her only daughter and child.

The girl yawned and rubbed sleep from her eyes. Nasula looked away and quickly wiped the tears from her face. The child must not see that she had been weeping. Sula was loving and caring. It always disturbed her to see her mother weeping.

'Mother, are you still not asleep till now? Is the night not moving towards dawn?'

'I will sleep.'

'That's what you have been saying. Mother, you will have a headache.'

'Sleep, child. What has woken you?'

'Come and sleep yourself.'

Sula threw the *citenge*, which had covered her when she'd been asleep, aside. This torn drab cloth was their only shield against the cold. Sula then gathered herself from the bare, tattered reed mat that was their bed and mattress and drew herself to her feet. She was of medium height, slender and beautiful.

Quietly, without undue haste, she unblocked the rickety straw door and lifted it to one side, leaning it against the wall. Nasula was relieved. She had thought Sula had risen to urge her to sleep and plead with her to stop worrying about their failure to find money for school fees. The child had often done this in the recent past and on every occasion it had been painful for both of them. She knew instead the reason that Sula had risen and wanted to stand up and escort her daughter, but she felt numb and decided to give her protection from where she was.

'Don't go far,' she said, 'just do it near there and be quick, it's too dark.'

'Uuh!'

11

'Just there, where are you going?'

Outside, not far from the door, water from the young one splattered. Nasula gazed out towards the wall of the hut beyond the hearth, thinking about her daughter. She loved the child with such an intensity that at times the feeling threatened to suffocate her. She did not want Sula to suffer the way she had done as an adult. She was too good-natured, well mannered, intelligent and hardworking.

The child entered the hut and replaced the straw door, then joined her mother by the fire.

Nasula did not ask her to go and sleep again. She did not want to disturb their emotions. Then she was suddenly seized by a strong feeling that she should tell her about her decision to travel to Mangano at sunrise that same day, to go and talk to Isaki and see if he could assist with the money for school.

So she let Sula settle down and then she told her. The child could not hold back her mind. She gave vent to her disapproval in a voice full of shock and pain. Did her mother seriously believe Isaki would give her anything? Why was her mother troubling herself? The Chiswebes with their farm had money, but it was their money. They were not going to part with a single coin to people they disrespected and hated as much as they disrespected and hated the two of them. What time had the Chiswebes for them?

'They don't know us.'

'What can I do?'

'If things have failed, mother, they have failed.'

'Let us sleep, it is nearing dawn.'

They lay down beside each other and pulled the *citenge* over themselves. The daughter slept. Nasula remained awake, slowly turning the heavy thoughts in her mind.

The Chiswebes at Mangano farm were selfish beings who loved money more than people. They were rough and glib-tongued. And they hated her for having refused to marry Isaki. But for her daughter, she would go and confront Isaki for money for Sula's school. Isaki was the one who was in charge of the farm. It was he who kept the money now that his father was getting very old.

Chapter Two

This is the way things end

These were the nineties. The late nineties. They were lean years. They were the years of each person for himself and hope only under the shadow of the gods. No one wanted to give because no one had anything to spare. The rains were bad and so the crops and the harvest were bad too. Without what to sell from the fields people had no money. Even chiefs and headmen who usually had a grain or two more than the ordinary people, roamed the land without an *ngwee* in hand. The days were truly hard.

The woman walked. She walked and walked, along a meandering footpath. Grains of sand in size and colour brought to her mind the sight and smell of roasted finger millet. The forest on both sides was dense, full of virginity, and a still silence as uncanny as that of the land of the dead. In that ghostly womb of untampered nature, the woman walked the distance to Mangano. Alone, unescorted by man. Nasula was courage. Days had inured her to many things and turned her into hard wood.

In the dead of the desertedness of the bush, the rhythmic sound of her feet and of grains of sand flying from under her oft-mended tropical sandals, produced frightening echoes that gave the illusion of some creature trailing her with evil intentions. But Nasula paid no attention to the menacing noise. She just moved on, her whole body and mind focused on the purpose of her journey. She was going to see Isaki for money for her daughter's schooling. That was all. Nothing else mattered.

Streams of sweat ran down her sides, soaking her worn, darkly coloured cotton dress and making her feel sticky. It was hot as not to be in May. She thought about the heat and gazed at the sky above with a questioning countenance. The height of the sun told her that it was noon and she realised that her stomach was empty and aching from hunger; and that she had not eaten anything the whole morning. She took out a piece of dried cassava and a handful of fried groundnuts from the sack-cloth bag hanging from a sisal string over her left shoulder and ate as she walked, not wanting to waste minutes resting at this time of the journey. The road ahead was still long and she must be in Mangano before the setting of the sun.

She must talk to Isaki today and know if Isaki would give her the money or not. Tomorrow she must return home and start doing whatever there would be to do, after she had received Isaki's answer. Time was not there. How many days were remaining before Sula was to be in class at the school where she had been selected to go for grade ten? What was the day today? Did she know the day today? The child had said today was Thursday. Today was Thursday. Two weeks and two days were remaining and how much time was that? On Monday, the week after the week after next week. That was when Sula was supposed to start classes.

If Isaki and his father would part with the money, she would have to rush back home to make arrangements to travel to Mbala with Sula: to go and buy a mattress, a blanket, bedsheets and other things on the list that the school authorities had sent of the things students must carry with them to the school. The trip to Mbala would be next week and Sula would start off for Kasama and St Theresa Girls Secondary School as early as possible the following week.

If the in-laws refused to part with the money? The gods forbid. That was not a question to ask. The idea of it was all the devils' horns and claws. She chased the thought away from her head into the forest and increased her step lest the question

15

catch up with her again. Nasula was determination. She was struggle and sacrifice. Her voice and spirit were not a voice and spirit soiled in pessimism. She would try anything and everything for the sake of her child's future, with faith in the gods.

Isaki and his father had spat on the ground, they had swept a finger across their necks and pointed to the sky and said she, Nasula, although she had been wife to the late Winelo, had stopped being one of them like the other people married, and to be married, into the Chiswebe family. They would not help her, even if they found her dying.

Inwardly, she too had vowed never to befriend any of them and chosen to perish with her poverty rather than accept a forced marriage and the wealth her dead husband had left her. She would not marry a man as lecherous as Isaki Chiswebe who already had three wives and had divorced the gods knew how many times before.

But that was many years ago when Sula had been just a little thing of five years of age. People changed with time and there was the future of an innocent child involved. Isaki and his father were not wild beasts. They must appreciate the good work she had done giving Sula schooling up to grade nine without any help from them. They must face the truth that Sula was their own blood and that the child herself had put in too much, seeing how far she had gone, to be neglected by them. They must see that the child was too intelligent and committed to her schooling to be wasted.

They must remember too that it was they who had taken everything the dead man had left behind. Had the dead man himself no eyes to see and be hurt?

She had decided and she was ready to fight. She would swallow her pride and brave the tide. She would go ahead and confront the Chiswebes and make them do that which they were obliged to do: produce money for the schooling of their granddaughter and niece, Sula. She had not been herself during the funeral of her late husband and in the years shortly thereafter. She had been too broken and weak for anything. Now she must face the lions and make them see the darkness of their deeds and the light ahead.

She had woken up before sunrise that morning. Sula had still been sleeping. As soon as she was up, she had rekindled the fire and roasted two pieces of dried cassava and fried two handfuls of groundnuts. After which she had taken her bag of sackcloth down from the wall, put the food and a piece of cotton cloth with which to tie whatever little thing she might be lucky to find on her way, into the bag, warmed water and washed her face, hands and legs.

Then she brought down her pair of tropical sandals, her only footwear, tied the straps where they had snapped with wires and slid her cracked feet into them. She only wore the sandals very rarely, on special occasions.

Going to Mangano today was no small thing. It meant going to the farm of rich people who were also in-laws. Above all, it meant going to see estranged relatives she had not seen since long back and ask them for money to give her daughter a future.

She had been feeling to see if the tropical sandals were holding well to her feet, alternatively raising them up and down where she was standing between the door and the fireplace, when Sula woke up.

'Where are you going?' Sula said, rising to her feet with the back of her right arm rubbing against her eyes. 'Mother, where is it that you are going?'

'I will be back here tomorrow.'

'It's not to Mangano that you are going, mother . . . or is it?'

'There is a little cassava meal in that calabash. A few of the beans we ate yesterday remain in the broken clay pot. The cassava meal will be enough for you for today and tomorrow.

But you know where the unpounded cassava is, if it happens that I don't return tomorrow. You can pound some of it for yourself. The cooked beans are enough for only one meal. When the sun rises, take some of the uncooked ones from the barn and cook enough for today and tomorrow.'

'Mother, why do you want to embarrass and trouble yourself for nothing?'

'I will find you.'

'Mother . . .'

'Don't keep yourself hungry for too long.'

Something rose within her like the wind before a heavy rain, and stirred her unsettled mind with new pain. She drew near to the daughter and passed her hand smoothly through the girl's long black hair.

'I will find you,' she said and walked out of the hut into the grey dusk of the morning, tears slipping down her cheeks. The journey to Mangano had started.

She had started on her way early in order to complete the most difficult part of it before it became dry and hot and the plaintive state of her stomach set in. The difficult part of the journey was the first half of the distance between Swelini, the home village, and Mangano. Mangano was to the west of Swelini and two streams before Senga Hill, which was along the tarred road from Mbala to Kasama.

The first half of the journey ended in Kuza village and formed the worst terrain of the journey with two treacherous ridges and a river. The next was Chitindi village. The way there was rough, undulating and over a ridge and two streams. After Chitindi, the land was generally flatter and densely covered with trees. Then, gradually, the land became more sparsely vegetated and began its slope towards Mangano.

Her step had been quick and strong when the air had been wet with mist and dew and she had been fresh. Now she was tired, hungry and thirsty. Her step was slower and weaker. Still, with the tenacity of a cheetah and the determination of a tortoise, Nasula tackled the distance steadily, surely, alone. At around midday, she calculated that she was likely to arrive at Mangano farm before four o'clock.

With the larger part of her journey behind her, tension and anxiety began to grip Nasula. It was painful to go to Mangano to see Isaki Chiswebe over money for Sula's schooling. She had not wanted such a thing to happen. She had wanted to raise the money through her own sweat or by borrowing from people she would pay or work for. But these were the nineties and the nineties were bad years. Nothing she had tried had worked. The path to Mangano was the only one left but every portion of it, every threat and danger that it posed, was inevitable.

The land became denuded of the dense forest and sloped towards her destination. The sun was riding low in the pale, clear sky. She joined the dust road from Senga Hill in the west to Chambeshi in the north east. The footpath from Swelini joined the road where the latter abandoned its easterly direction and curved to the north east. Walking in the middle of the road where it was flat, she continued with her journey, her mind too much in turmoil for her to be aware of her aching muscles, the cracking of thirst in her throat and the hunger in the pit of her stomach.

She entered the first scattered outskirts of Chilwazo, the village within whose domain lay Mangano farm, and the story of the misery of the nineties lay before her, as it had done when she had passed through other villages, and as it seemed it always was in Swelini, her own village: badly devastated crops, scorched land, a loud, stringent air of lifelessness: Why did it care to rain now, in May, at the end of its season, when it had refused to do so when it mattered most, between October and March?

These, truly, were not years. No, they were not years. They were the evil breath of a world turned upon itself. Everywhere streams and rivers were drying from the land. Streams and rivers that had always overflowed with water since the beginning of time. Some were reduced to mud while others were just dry sand where birds and animals played or scratched for food. The lakes, they too, were going. Those who returned from Mbala and Mpulungu were saying Chila was half its size, the rest had become dry land; and Lake Tanganyika had sunk so low that even a baby could see what had happened.

The village of Chilwazo was such a distance to the right of the road to Senga Hill that it was not visible. You could only tell where it was from the smoke that hung above it and the hushed noise from its people and their livestock. The woman by-passed the village without meeting anyone. She liked it that way.

She had escaped the punishment of answering questions about where she was going, what she was going to do, where she had been all that long time, what she had been doing, and life and death. The people of Chilwazo were of the devil. Gossip was what they broke their fast with, lunched and suppered on. They would put a load on your head, which you would fail to lift down even up to the day you went to your grave.

Chilwazo village was far behind. A dust road, smaller than the one to Senga Hill, appeared on the left going in a south-westerly direction. She turned into the road and, after a short distance, came to Chitulamilongo, the small stream that formed the northern boundary of Mangano farm and had once poured its water into the much larger stream Yande in the west. Was this Chitulamilongo, the fast, noisy snake of running water? Who could believe it? The stream was a silent, motionless bed of dry sand, twigs and leaves. The jungle was still lush but the ground was dry, cracked and hard. Turning thoughts of disbelief in her head, she walked along the two logs that formed the bridge across Chitulamilongo and left the stream, hastily, afraid of relating the sight of these things to the fate of things ahead of her.

The road now headed directly south. A forest of wild trees, then that of trees planted by man, and she had arrived. She felt shock, her very first glance told it all. Mangano farm had fallen from prosperity to poverty and squalor. There was dilapidation and unkemptness everywhere her eyes settled as she traversed the farm's village on the way to the main house; the May air, brittle with the tension of woe and suffering, held a stillness that smelt of death.

The dogs were bones, the chickens so few they seemed not to exist, and there was not a single goat, pig, duck or guinea fowl in sight. No cattle, no sheep, no pigeons. Yet in the past these had formed part of an over-flowing life of prosperity that greeted your eyes, nose and ears the moment you entered the farm. The kraal had collapsed, rotten and overgrown with grass and small trees. The furrow that passed through the village, from the *dambo* in the south-east to the garden in the west, lay dry and overgrown with various small plants. The fish ponds too, to the south, which had once been fed with water from the furrow, were no more.

The main house, where the old man Chiswebe lived with his first wife and the youngest children and some of his grand-children, was at the southern end of the farm's village. This was a big white house with glass windows and a roof of iron sheets, facing east; slightly to the south east was the kitchen, a one-roomed brick building with a thatched roof facing north.

Apart from the old man's house there was only one other building in the village which had an iron roof, glass windows, and walls that were plastered and painted. This was Isaki Chiswebe's house, a low, wide building painted blue and situated in the north-eastern corner of the village. The rest had

21

thatched roofs and were made from stakes and mud or bricks, and were situated before the main house on either side of the road as you were coming from Senga Hill.

Devoured by curiosity and premonition, Nasula entered the grounds of the patriarch's home. No one saw her arrive and she saw no one. The homestead was as quiet and lifeless as a graveyard at night. At the front door of the main house, opposite the kitchen, she stopped walking and stood in silence for a while, listening and wondering.

Then she called: 'Ohdi!' A coarse voice responded faintly and its owner, a tall shrivelled old woman with a rugged face and deep, misty eyes came out of the kitchen followed by a small boy and two equally small girls.

It was her mother-in-law, Chiswebe's first wife Nakulukili.

Kili, the granddaughter, by whose name the mother-in-law was called, was the eldest daughter and first-born of Kwesela the eldest daughter and second child of Chiswebe after Winelo. Kili herself was married and had children. Winelo had married late, at the age of thirty-five. That was why Sula, his first-born and only child, was only fifteen.

'Is this not Nasula of ours!' exclaimed Nakulukili on recognising the just arrived. 'Are my own eyes cheating me? Am I getting so old that I see wrongly in full daylight? What good you have done to come. Nasula of ours? Welcome *mama*!'

Jovial words, but there was not a hint of gaiety in the voice or face. Both spoke of a life drained of sap and capable only of the tale of sorrow and suffering. Nasula began to walk towards the old woman: mother-in-law and daughter-in-law met and greeted each other.

Nakulukili then lifted the bag of sackcloth from Nasula's shoulder and went back into the kitchen saying she was going to bring out the stools so they could sit outside where there was no smoke.

Nasula turned to the small ones and shook hands with each one of them, enquiring about their health and schooling. The children too were a tale of the bad days at Mangano. They were dusty, thin and hungry-looking, their sad little faces blemished with the saltpetre of dried tears.

Nakulukili returned from the kitchen with two carved stools and the two women sat down together in the shadow of the kitchen, facing the main house. The small ones, at Nakulukili's request, went to tell the other people at the farm that Nasula from Swelini had come.

'Is father present?' Nasula asked, impatient to clear her fear that the old man Chiswebe and his son Isaki, with whom she would discuss her problem, might be away. 'And brother-in-law Isaki?'

'They are present both of them,' Nakulukili said with such melancholy in her voice that a chill seeped into Nasula's stomach and she shifted on her stool. 'Shikulukili is sleeping and Isaki is at his home.'

The conversation stumbled from subject to subject, Sula being the most prominent among issues. Other people and their visitors came and greeted Nasula and chatted with her before going back. And in the course of things Nasula came to learn about the long illness of Isaki Chiswebe.

Two years had passed with Isaki in and out of hospital in Mbala, coughing and, recently, suffering from diarrhoea. Six months ago the hospital staff had given up and refused to keep him there saying he would be better off looked after in his home. But his condition was worsening with each day that passed and now he could neither talk nor move his limbs.

His third and second wife had since died of a similar illness that started with coughing and was followed by diarrhoea. They had both lost the youngest of their children through death from malignant sores and diarrhoea before falling ill for long periods

23

and dying. The first and only surviving wife was no longer very healthy either.

Nasula was speechless where she sat. There was not what to say or think. She was lost and confused. She had come to the hearth of the fallen and dying where, clearly, nothing existed to fight or fight for. Where the remaining flicker of life and living itself beckoned for help and sympathy. Where there was no sign of hope for her and her problem. Her journey to Mangano had not the colour of a journey to salvation.

Those coming to greet and see her stopped coming. She was suddenly alone sitting by the kitchen. Nakulukili was back inside cooking. Nasula rested a little more. Then she rose, and standing by the door, told Nakulukili that she was going to see the sick man.

'See him and come back and rest from here,' the old woman said, beating off the smoke from the fireplace with her hand. 'It is a long journey you have travelled. Swelini is not a small distance. Do not punish yourself staying long.'

'I will be back,' Nasula said and began to walk to Isaki Chiswebe's house. Her body was stiff with fatigue, her feet heavy with tiredness, and the hunger in her belly excruciating. Not a morsel of anything had been offered to her to eat by anybody. She understood. In the past, it would have been different. Foods would have been offered her from everywhere and by everybody before she settled down. This time, there was no food. She understood and had said nothing about the condition of her stomach to anybody. She had only asked for water to drink and what she had been given had been so muddy it had failed to quench her thirst.

'We scratch it from ponds along the Yande,' Nakulukili had explained; 'the stream itself is just mud, people walk in it daily in search of fish, the water hardly moves.'

'This is what is happening in Swelini and everywhere.'

'It is a sad way of the world coming to an end.'

A small crowd of tense-looking men and women was gathered in the dusty patch of ground fronting Isaki Chiswebe's house. Nasula bowed to the crowd on arriving and entered the house without saying anything to them. In the sitting-room, three women she recognised only as villagers of Chilwazo, were sitting on the floor in the corner on her immediate left, two of them dozing and the other one breast-feeding her baby. There had been chairs and other furniture in the sitting-room in the past, but there was not a single piece of furniture in sight now. She brought her hands together and bowed to the women in greeting and proceeded into the bedroom on her right and towards which the women were facing.

Darkness, a deathly stink and stuffiness swallowed her as she entered the room. Then the pungent smell of freshly boiled, burnt and crushed herbs and roots; of rotting solutions of concoctions prepared a long time ago but not used; of medicines from the hospital; of stale human breath and excretion; and of burning charcoal. She halted and stood in silence until her eyes became used to the darkness in the room and she could see properly.

She had imagined finding Isaki Chiswebe lying huge and long on a high bed of metal and wood. There was neither a bed nor a corpulent figure in the room. A thin, torn, filthy, foam mattress was what she saw instead, spread sadly along the eastern wall. On it lay a dark blanket gathered around what looked like a narrow log beaten flat, at the southern end of which a pale human head, dark and shrivelled, lay on a mound of old, torn clothes wrapped in a shredded *citenge*. Blood ran to her head in waves of horror. Could this be Isaki Chiswebe?

The world is fire. It can burn a life to nothing. This was Isaki Chiswebe, finished, shrunk to a stick in a lifeless, wrinkled skin, ridden with sores and pimples. His lips, excoriated, burned a pale crimson and his once protruding dark eyes were sunken and glazed in their deep, ditch-like sockets that made his long, bony face appear hollow.

The space between where the mattress ended (a little beyond the feet of the sick man) and the northern wall was covered with dishes, gourds and tins containing medical waters for, it seemed, washing the sick man and steaming him. Sitting on a carved, three-legged stool and leaning against the northern wall, a sinewy old woman wearing a dark dress, larger than her size, made of *citenge* material, was rinsing her hands with a rag. Opposite her and leaning against the southern wall next to an array of bottles, cups and plates containing medicines and crumbs of food, which the sick man must have failed to eat, sat Emeliya the first wife of Isaki Chiswebe. She was hunched before a brazier in which there was a fire covered in ash. It was not cold, but she was warming herself. After a second look and recognising her, Nasula saw that Emeliya too was very ill and her once fat, robust body now looked frail and pale, shrunk to less than half of its original size. Nasula greeted Emeliya and then the old woman. She did not know the old woman and Emeliya did not explain her. So Nasula concluded that she was a herbalist.

Nasula pulled up the stool that Emeliya pushed towards her and, after looking around, sat down before the sick man between Emeliya and the old woman.

'Father of Bupe,' she said, meaning to call the sick man and gazing at him, her heart suddenly bleeding with pity and fear; 'Father of Bupe, it is me, Nasula.'

'He will not answer,' the old woman said to her, in a low, husky voice.

'He does not talk,' added Emeliya, coughing a long dry cough that would not leave her and made her shake violently, her voice seeming to jerk between spasms.

26

The rest of her time in the room – and Nasula remained there for quite a long time – passed without the sick man moving any part of his body, a deathly stillness of flesh. The inevitable act of breathing caused feeble, monotonous movements of his chest; and the only sound he produced was a weak, groan-like noise in the throat and, occasionally, a faint dry cough. Nasula did not talk again. She only watched the sick man and reeled with horror at the thought of what would have been had she agreed to marry Isaki after the death of Winelo.

Nobody had told her, but she knew. She could tell what it was, the disease that had afflicted Isaki and his three wives. It was the new, unmentionable disease of the world that came of the taste of flesh, the one that made you thin before taking you, the disease of today.

Had the wealth that Winelo had left behind attracted her into a forced marriage, she too would have picked the disease from Isaki and gone the way his second and third wife had gone, and the way Isaki was going and his first wife would soon go. Nasula would have left Sula behind, poor and alone in the world, while the child was still very young. The gods forbid!

She did not converse with the other women in the room. The old woman dozed and Emeliya, it seemed, avoided talking so as not to provoke her cough.

'Let me leave you now, I will go and see if father has woken up. We have not greeted each other yet, he and I,' Nasula said at last and drew her feet backwards in readiness.

'He usually rises as the sun is about to set,' responded Emeliya; the harsh, sore, throatiness of her voice chilled Nasula. 'He is here throughout the night. We take over from him during the day, mother Nakulukili and myself. Go and see, he could be up.'

The cough seized her in a storm. She heaved and shook and choked. One of her feet hit the brazier and caused a cloud of ashes to cascade to the floor, and led to a crescendo of coughing.

Weakly, she picked up a rag from beside her, and spat into the rag. She stopped coughing, wiped her mouth and put the rag down.

'Go and greet him.'

'We will see each other again.'

The old woman had started snoring. Nasula stood up. The end of one of the wires with which the straps of her tropical sandals had been mended pricked her foot. She bent down and folded the end of the wire away from her body. Then she turned and left the room and the house. Stiffened with fatigue, hunger, thirst, horror and hopelessness, she traversed the parched grounds of the dying farm.

The sun was slowly crouching down behind the horizon to shelter from the miseries of the earth, the twilight of the occasion blurring everything with a bloody red dusk. She entered the yard of the main house and was about to go into the kitchen when the door of the main house creaked and opened. She saw the old man Chiswebe coming out of the house, a collapsible wooden chair in his hands. She turned and walked slowly towards him, a sad dwindling old man with a crumpled look clothed in a dusty black suit.

When she greeted him, he blinked stressfully then his big dark eyes, dry as old *kaponda* leaves, peered into the twilight at her and he exclaimed in happy recognition.

'Lunga,' he called, after he had greeted Nasula, 'bring a stool for your sister-in-law here.'

He unfolded the chair he was carrying and placed it near the wall of the house, not far north of the doorstep. Then he stood waiting for Lunga, a boy of about fourteen years, his last-born, to bring a stool for her. When the stool was handed to Nasula, the old man lowered himself into the chair and sat down facing the kitchen. Nasula seated herself at a distance in front of him and to his left.

'You travelled well on your journey?' he asked.

'Except the tiredness.'

'Swelini is a distance.'

His voice was accepting, welcoming and sorry. Polite, compassionate and fatherly, calling for sympathy and forgiveness. The old tone of pompousness and authority was completely gone. Every morsel of his being was evidence of a famished man whom tribulation had withered from a colossus to an ordinary human being, so that now he sat awkward and uncertain before her, shrouded in doubt, attempting to cling to the cloak of an old dignity that had grown thin in the last sad years.

She could feel it sadly even as she stole furtive glances of him; there was no need to tell the old man about her problem. With Isaki having been sick for the past two years, nothing had happened at the farm for a long time; and from the way everything and everybody appeared, the one hundred thousand *kwacha* she needed for Sula's schooling was too much money for anyone to find, let alone spare.

But when the old man enquired about Sula's health and schooling, she could not restrain herself. She forgot about everything and explained her problem and the purpose of her journey to him.

'What to do for the child, my grand-daughter, Sula of the rains, wretched world,' the old man lamented. 'She has passed very well to go to such a good school, while we have become empty-handed and as good as dead. How unfortunate the child is. What a shame!'

Two years ago, he said, sombrely, they had taken a fertiliser loan with Isaki from an agent of Cavmont Merchant Bank and the government. The harvest was not good. They failed to repay the loan fully. In the meantime Isaki fell sick and they failed to grow anything the following year. Then the agent came and collected everything of value from the farm: livestock, furniture, crops, everything. And that was it, the beginning of the farm's slow death and suffering. Now they had nothing, not even an *ngwee* with which to buy soap.

It was true. Nasula had eyes to see. Chiswebe had become a man who washed without soap. His once shiny, soap-smooth skin was coarsened and dull. His appearance had changed greatly and he had aged. He looked like an old man. His shoulders once heavy and straight had sagged and shrunk; his round face had elongated; his hair had turned so white that its earlier black and grey streaks had vanished.

These were the nineties, the years when there was a harshness and hardness in the land that had little sympathy for the weak. New people were in government and the sons and daughters of the land were breathing with a new spirit. Borrow to pay back, not to steal, they were saying. A good spirit. A person must pay for what she or he borrows and work hard for what she or he eats. But when the rain is bad and the crop is bad as a result, what can a person do?

In the past borrowing was thieving. People borrowed fertiliser, seed and farm implements and refused to pay when even a child could see the rain and the crop had been good. But now borrowing was digging your own grave. If the rain frowned upon you and the sun scorched your crop into failure, they made you pay with your blood.

The nineties were difficult years. They were the years of money first or else no friendship. And they were the years when the new disease of the world, the advent of the eighties, decided to sit down on a stool by the riverside and fish people like *cisense*.

They were not years to scratch your head or yield to the next flesh you ran into. They were dangerous years. Hard and poisonous.

The darkness thickened, swallowing the twilight and everything into its belly. Supper was ready. Nasula was called into the kitchen. The food was so little, it was *nshima* with boiled monkey-nuts, and the people to eat it so many that her hunger was hardly touched. The plates were empty before she could settle down. The water to drink too. There was not enough of it and it was too muddy. Her thirst was touched but it remained unquenched.

She was shown a room to sleep in, in one of Isaki Chiswebe's smaller houses, a small house of burnt bricks with a thatched roof, one of two similar houses to the north of the main house. It was the house in which Isaki's third wife had lived. The house was now occupied by a young sister of Chiswebe who, at thirty, was as yet unmarried but had a daughter who was eight years old. A reed mat and two *citenge* were put on the floor of the room for Nasula to use. After supper, she went to the sick man's home and stayed there for some time before going back to sleep.

The shadow of failure loomed over her as she lay waiting for sleep to come. She did not know what to do next to save Sula's schooling. What must she do to raise one hundred thousand *kwacha* for the child? Sadness and remorse gripped her like a fever. Late into the night, she talked to herself, mournfully regretting having insisted on coming to Mangano, bitterly blaming herself for failing to provide for the child, and cursing herself for having married a man who would be killed stealing paint and leave her suffering with a child to look after.

'What shall I do, people of the world?' she said. 'This is the way things end: this could be the end of my daughter's schooling, I say it!'

◆

She was suddenly in a hurry to go back to Swelini, to the familiar atmosphere of home, to see what other ideas the gods might breathe into her. There was no time to waste. But remembering the seriousness of Isaki's illness, she reasoned that it would not be a good gesture for her to leave without spending at least one whole day at the farm. So she decided to leave very early in the morning on Saturday and spend Friday at the farm.

As the day broke on Saturday, Isaki Chiswebe died. She could not leave before the burial and one more day of mourning.

Isaki was buried that same day in the afternoon. On Sunday, she excused herself to Chiswebe and Nakulukili that she had left Sula alone and without much food; and that the time to find money for the child's schooling was nearly over and suggested she depart very early on Monday. She bade them goodbye before going to sleep. As the sky was beginning to redden early on Monday morning, she woke up and began her journey back to Swelini. Nothing had been given her, not even something to eat or drink on the way: she knew and understood it was not out of ill intention.

Chapter Three

When light streaks the sky, hope begins to burn

'Was it a person that we buried, child of mine? Sula, are you not just hearing it from me, another person, who was there? Would you have looked there a second time, my daughter?' The woman clapped her hands incredulously after the words.

'You are just hearing about it,' she said again, whetting her daughter's curiosity further. 'My daughter, it was a semblance of a person that we buried. A dry stalk of *musanze*, if you ask. He was like this!'

She brought the forefinger of her left hand between the forefinger and the thumb of her right hand and twisted it to show the daughter what she meant.

'A young one like you would not have known it was the same Isaki Chiswebe you have always known lying there where he lay. To die many times over would be better than to die one single death like that. These are things you who are beginning to know the world now should see and learn from when the sun is still shining. When your mother says the world has teeth and tells you to be with legs crossed wherever you are, you think she has not what to say.'

The daughter looked down and smiled shyly.

'You are laughing?' Nasula said, smiling herself. 'Are you any more a baby, there where you are now? Have you not already entered the dangerous period? Is it not you who was telling me about Polo son of Maselino Kapapi not long ago and what he says about you being beautiful and wanting to marry you in future? Where does playful talk like that lead? And do

33

you know where death like the death Isaki died from comes from?'

'I know.'

'You know? So you know. It would kill me to see my own daughter and only child running into a death like that out of carelessness. Don't just say "I know". Learn also to be a house with a lock without a key. When time ripens, the spirits will nod and the gods will provide the key and tell you to open the door.'

'You buried him on Sunday?'

'We buried him the day before yesterday, Saturday. Today is Monday or is it not?'

'It is Monday.'

'Yes, we buried him the day before yesterday. I would have stayed to mourn a while longer, but I thought of the way I had left you and also the days remaining before the time you are supposed to report for school. I decided to excuse myself and come back today.'

They were in front of their hut. The daughter was pounding cassava in a carved mortar, standing with her back to the hut; and the mother, sitting on a flat carved stool, was sieving the pounded cassava into a dish and throwing what did not go through the sieve into a straw basket, on her immediate right. The sun was low, but some distance from the end of the sky; the world was growing cool but still in full daylight. A soft wind was blowing.

It was not long since Nasula had arrived from Mangano. She had come torn like a cloth with tiredness, hunger and thirst; with disappointment, fear and horror. The moment she had arrived, buried in a cocoon of perspiration, Sula, without being told or asking, had bustled about and made her *nshima* and served it to her with beans and *pupwe*. These were the ways of Sula, the ways of hard work, initiative and responsibility to herself and other people: the ways of intelligence, sensitivity and wisdom.

Even as she had been eating, Nasula had thought about her daughter and imagined how the child must have taken every moment seriously, doing this and that in readiness for her return. And the child had sat nearby and watched her eat, passing her what she needed: a plate, water, salt and so on.

What about the journey to Mangano? How had things gone? What was the outcome of the effort? Sula did not ask and she was not going to ask. Sula was a delicate young soul who was able to see through things and understand the frailty of them like an adult, not just any adult, a good one who knew well where and when not to open a mouth. Stealing glances at the girl as she ate, from what she saw and knew about her, Nasula was convinced the child knew that things had not gone well at Mangano, and that she had come back empty-handed. Yet she was convinced too that the child would not ask her about the matter.

A solemn silence between them, mother and daughter sat in the middle of their hut, between the hearth and the sleeping place, talking to each other only through the movements of their eyes and bodies. After she had finished eating, Nasula lay down on the reed mat at their sleeping place and slept, speechless and confused from the pangs of tiredness and unsuccessfulness.

She felt better after she had eaten, downed half a gourd of water and slept for quite some time. She had woken up at the sound of pestle and mortar fighting and found it was Sula pounding cassava and joined her.

'You have rested enough already?'

'*Ee.*'

'You were dying when you just arrived.'

'The distance, hunger, thirst and the heat of this May which is not May but October.'

'You didn't carry much to eat on the way?'

'Did I carry a single grain of what to eat with me? What and from where, child of mine? Do you think Mangano is still Mangano? Are we worse into hunger and suffering than the people of Mangano? My child? *Iye mwe!*'

'What has happened to all that wealth of theirs?'

'Was it not in the past that people got free things from the government and went about looking like rich people over things for which they had not dropped a single bead of sweat? Do you think things are the same with these new people in government? The fertiliser people they failed to pay, came and took away every wealth that Mangano farm was made of, from what to sleep on, to the last animal!'

'*Owe!*'

'Your grandfather now looks like a tramp bitten by a snake and waiting to die.'

'You can laugh as if it is a good thing that has happened. The way you say it, mother!'

'Do you think I am adding lies to the truth? My daughter you are just hearing it from me. You should have seen it with your own eyes. Whoever has said these years are years of a new day has not told a lie. The world has swallowed a poisonous toad.'

She went on and told the daughter more about the grandfather, Sikulukili Chiswebe, and how badly Mangano farm had fallen. That was when she had turned to Isaki Chiswebe's long illness and death. Now a consuming tension swept through her like a wave, the tension of obligation to tell Sula the outcome of her journey, concerning the money for the child's schooling.

'It was no use even going there for your money for school,' she said, her whole being throbbing with pain. 'They could not produce even a coin and they didn't have it.'

'Don't worry, it's all right,' said Sula, her beautiful brown eyes caressing her mother with a warm, sympathetic stare. 'I will not be the first or last person to stop schooling because of lack of money.'

'Child, don't talk like that . . .'

'They were lucky, those who went to school in the sixties, seventies and eighties, when education was not paid for and everything needed was provided free. Now in the nineties, things are different, and we must accept what is happening to us. It won't help even if we complain and grieve. Who will listen to us?'

'I say stop talking like that.'

'If we have tried and failed . . . ?'

'You must go to school. You can't stop your schooling just like that. Do you not feel sorry for yourself? Do you not see how we are suffering because I did not go to school? You want your future to be like this?'

'Mother, I understand, but . . .'

'You must go to school. You don't know what suffering I have gone through because apart from being poor and a woman, my parents did not send me to school. I don't want you to suffer the way I have suffered. I want you to grow up to stand on your own feet and not look to marriage or men for salvation. Marriage and men are not salvation but the ruin of any woman who can't stand on her own feet. I want you to go far with your education so that you can support yourself, earn a good living and be free and independent in your life. You must go to school!'

'But how, mother? Where are you going to get one hundred thousand *kwacha* from in the little time left before I am supposed to report for school? For how long have you been trying, and where have you not gone and what have you not done but failed? Don't you feel sorry for yourself?'

Nasula, now in a state of distress, was silent. The words from her daughter felt like rocks falling from afar, blows to her

37

consciousness. Sula, that child, was another one. The power of her word would knock down an elephant. Yes, how was she, her mother, to send her to school without money? Where was she going to find one hundred thousand *kwacha* in the next seven or so days when she had been trying and failing to raise the money for the past more than one year?

Wishing, she thought, can eat away a person's sanity and wisdom. Nasula, how do you insist the child must go to school when you have not the faintest idea if and where you can find the money to pay for the schooling? Come to think of it, Nasula, woman, are you not going mad?

More than a year and a half ago, when Sula had completed grade eight, Nasula had thought about what would happen when she finished grade nine, when Sula passed and went on to grade ten. She had seen as early as this, that in just about a year's time, she would need a lot of money to send Sula to a bigger and more senior school as there was no grade ten, eleven and twelve at Senga Hill Basic School. She had panicked and started thinking of what she should do to prepare the money, and enough of it, in time. It was then that the fertiliser agent was lending out fertiliser at Senga Hill for that year's farming season. An idea crossed Nasula's mind. She should borrow fertiliser and maize seed and grow maize. When she asked about how one borrowed from the fertiliser agent, she found out that she would not qualify. Her field was too small and she had no money to pay the deposit the agent was asking for.

She did not give up. She talked to a villager of Swelini who had managed to borrow from the fertiliser agent and convinced him to give her a bit of what he had received, at a repayment that would be more than what the agent would ask for from the villager at harvesting time. The villager, Pupila was his name, gave her two pockets: one D-compound for basal dressing and one Urea for top dressing. He also gave her, on credit, half of a small-size pocket of seed maize.

It was agreed that she would repay Pupila two and a half ninety kilogram bags of maize for one pocket of fertiliser, and half a bag of maize for the half pocket of seed. Which meant five and a half bags of maize altogether. The agent was asking for two bags of maize for one pocket of fertiliser and was selling the seed for cash. Pupila would therefore give the agent four bags and keep one bag and a half for himself. Pupila would collect the maize from her as soon as she had harvested the maize sometime in July the following year.

Together and alone with her daughter, she toiled and toiled. With attention to every detail of timing, application and tending her field, she managed to plant all the seed, apply fertiliser and weed it. But the rains were not enough. The idea had been to harvest eleven bags of maize, give five and a half to Pupila, use half a bag, and keep five for selling in April, at a time when there would be a serious shortage of maize, and just a month before Sula would be due to leave for school, at not less than twenty thousand *kwacha* a bag. Instead, she had harvested a paltry six bags of bad grain and Pupila, who refused to understand what had happened, wrested all his five and a half bags from her and left her with only half a bag, which only lasted a couple of months as a source of mealie meal for her and her daughter.

She tried to raise the money by doing piece work. It couldn't work. The people she approached to do work for would promise her money, which she clearly stated was what she needed for her daughter's schooling, at the time of negotiating. But once she had done the work for them, they would plead being coinless and pay her in kind, things that no one could buy if she tried to sell them. An old plate, *pupwe*, a basket, cassava or a rag.

Disappointed and frustrated, she stopped and started trying to borrow money which she could then work for over months or pay back in the form of produce or money itself during the next harvesting season. That too failed. No one wanted to lend because no one was in a position to lend. There was no money around, and she was too poor to be trusted.

In November, she cried to Pupila again. The man gave her two pockets of fertiliser and a half pocket of seed maize, and again she toiled and planted the half pocket of seed maize. But this being May, just over five months after she had sowed the seed, which was a late maturing seed, the crop was not yet ready for harvesting, and even if it had been, Pupila would not have allowed her to sell any of it before he collected his share first, especially because the rain and the crop were again not good and no one could tell how much was to be harvested from her field.

Sula stopped pounding and put the pestle down on the ground. Sweating, she tilted the mortar towards a plastic dish. When the mouth of the mortar was near the mouth of the dish, she scooped the cassava from the mortar into the dish with a swift right hand while holding the mortar in place with the left hand. Through with that, she stood the mortar back in its upright position, lifted the basket where her mother had poured the cassava solids that had not gone through the sieve and poured some of its contents back into the mortar. She then picked the pestle from the ground, but instead of starting to pound the cassava in the mortar again, she merely planted one end of the pestle in the mortar and held the other end against her shoulder and exclaimed, 'Mother, I have remembered. Why did I forget?' she said, glad to be raising a different issue. Money for her schooling was always an emotional subject which upset her mother. 'There is a woman of Wimbe village who lives in Lusaka who came to Wimbe for a funeral. She is here in Swelini.

She came to visit her in-laws, the family of Yowani Sikalumbi. She came yesterday and will be returning to Wimbe tomorrow before going back to Lusaka sometime this week. She says she knows you from Lusaka.'

'A woman of Wimbe village who lives in Lusaka?'

'We met at the well when I went to draw water in the morning. She recognised me and remembered you because I look like you, that's what she said. She called me Sula, before I told her my name, and told me I was the daughter of Belita Bowa, the wife of the late Winelo Chiswebe. She knows you so well. Did I laugh, mother, she even mentioned another name, a nickname, of yours, one that you have never told me about.'

Nasula smiled, her face brightening slightly.

'Are you not mad, laughing at your mother's name?'

'It sounded funny and it doesn't suit you. It's a name that would suit someone who is unruly. Pantoka. *Iye!*'

They laughed: both of them. Pantoka!

'Your great-grandmother, my grandmother Chitanti, from my father's side, gave it to me at birth. She said she thought of it because I was born a baby that was in the habit of kicking my legs about.'

'And when you grew up, you stopped kicking your legs about and forgot about the name, and to tell me that you had once been called Pantoka?'

'I have now told you, if you like the name, keep it in your head so that you can remember it later and give it to one of your granddaughters.'

'If there will be one who will be in the habit of kicking her legs about?'

'You ask me? You will be the grandmother to decide, not me.

'Sula, how did she look, the woman? Why do you let us talk about small silly things when you have brought up something serious and important to talk about?'

'She is shorter but wider than you. Darker, with a wide gap between her front teeth. Very jovial and friendly.'

Nasula shrugged the doubt off herself. The woman her memory had captured must be the one. That the woman had a wide gap between her front teeth and was very jovial and friendly had done it. Who else that she knew in Lusaka could be of these parts?

'Let it not be Nalukwi.'

'That's what she said I should tell you her name was. I have remembered now. She said she would come here in the evening to see if you would be back from Mangano because she will be leaving for Wimbe very early in the morning tomorrow.'

'And you didn't remember her yourself?'

'Not a bit.'

'She used to carry you on her back every time we happened to be together with her, in Lusaka. She used to come to our home in Kalingalinga compound from Chaisa compound. She liked you very much and you liked her too, but you were too small to have remembered her, and she came home only once in a while.'

Nasula began to feel nervous. The knowledge of Nalukwi's presence in the village made her feel nervous with anticipation. The coming of Nalukwi to Swelini and her home might bring an answer to her problem of money for school for Sula.

Nalukwi was a poor, older acquaintance of hers, one who could not have as much as a hundred thousand *kwacha* to spare or a good portion of it. But she knew her as a wonderful woman who was sympathetic, helpful and given to providing timely answers to others in times of difficulty.

When Winelo Chiswebe had died, Nalukwi had acted as someone who was her own relative during and after the funeral. She had sat and stood next to her through it all, consoling her and holding her in place.

When the Chiswebe family and relatives arrived at the funeral

42

house and no one came from Nasula's side, as she had no one in the world to do so, Nalukwi organised her own friends, relatives and village friends to stand by Nasula and represent her to the family of the deceased and answer their incessant queries and demands. Nalukwi herself spoke for her in everything. She saw to it that Nasula was not harassed into talking unnecessarily, that she spoke only to her and through her most of the time, and that no one was allowed to speak directly to Nasula except through her or with her permission. Without her and her tenacity and strength, Nasula would have been harangued to her own death by the Chiswebe family over the death of Winelo Chiswebe.

She was not there when the Chiswebes were throwing Nasula out of the house Winelo had left. But when she met Nasula at Kamwala bus station, a month after Nasula had become homeless and was, together with the child, Sula, spending nights at the bus station because she had no money for transport to travel back to the village, she had taken the woman to her home and looked after her while questing for a way to help her find the money she needed to go home to Swelini.

Within a week, through a farm-worker friend of hers, she found her piece work at one of the big farms along the road to Kafue where Nasula worked for two months and made enough money for her bus fare to Senga Hill and the other things she needed.

To Nasula, Nalukwi was a miracle woman who was a glow of inspiration and reassurance, a poor struggling woman who turned things that were heavier than rock into adventures, each lighter than a dry leaf. Remembering her grace and knowing she was in the village, Nasula had a feeling something in the direction of salvation and hope was about to happen. Silently but with a zeal that burned red like a coal, she prayed to the gods not to turn what was happening into a dream.

43

'You are sure, Sula, the woman said she was Nalukwi?'

'She said she was Nalukwi and I heard one of the daughters of Yowani Sikalumbi, whom she came with to the well, call her Nalukwi.'

'You also heard well that she said she would be coming here to our home today in the evening to see if I would be back from Mangano?'

'She said it many times. She talked to me for a long time, people at the well were surprised at the way she talked to me and how happy she looked to have met me.'

'That can only be Nalukwi. It is she that you met, child. The woman of a woman. If she does not come, I will go to the home of Yowani Sikalumbi myself, to see her. But knowing Nalukwi, she will come. I am sure she will come. Nalukwi?'

Sula started pounding the cassava in the mortar. Nasula shifted on the stool, excitement and anxiety growing to full bloom inside her. A flicker of an idea: What to do for Nalukwi? The thought came unbidden. From habit, she stopped sieving and stared thoughtfully into the distance, her sad, brown eyes active.

'Sula, stop what you are doing,' she said suddenly; 'be quick, child, chase that chicken and catch it immediately. We must kill it for Nalukwi.'

'Ah, mother, what are you saying?' Sula said, genuinely surprised at her mother's decision. 'Do you know how many chickens we are remaining with after those two died on their own?'

'I say be quick.'

'One cock, one cockerel and two chickens. The rest are week-old chicks and they too are only five.'

'For Nalukwi, even if there had been only one, I would have killed it for her. Child, have I ever told you the story of what I went through with you in Lusaka after your father died and how in the end I managed to come back here to the village?'

'No.'

'I have thought of doing so when you reach the age of eighteen. Now you are still too young for the story. That is why I have never remembered Nalukwi to you. It would have forced me to say other things about my past, things that are not good food for a young innocent mind like yours. For the time being just know that without Nalukwi, you and me might not be here today. Do you hear me?'

'I do, mother.'

'Be quick, go and catch that chicken. We will kill it now. Time has gone already. Nalukwi will be arriving at any time. I know that woman and how she is. She can't fail to come.'

Sula put the pestle down on the ground. She spotted, on her mother's head, a small tuft of smoke-darkened grass from the roof of the hut, blown there by the wind. She went up to her mother and, standing by her side, facing the direction the mother was facing, she removed the fleck from her mother's head, showed it to her and threw it away. Then she turned and started towards a speckled white and black chicken, which was resting in the shadow of a rickety barn, south of the hut. At her approach, and as she drew near, the chicken ran away clucking. Sula took chase.

Nasula put the sieve away in the basket and went and picked several sticks of firewood from a heap behind the hut. Inside, she broke the sticks into pieces, putting each broken piece on to the fireplace. Next, she poured water from a gourd into a clay pot and placed the clay pot on the tripod of stones round the fire. Then she fanned the fire aflame with her breath and sat back coughing, thick smoke billowing from the fireplace.

The fire blazed. The smoke cleared. The chicken Sula was

45

chasing ran into the hut and hid between the gourd containing water and the wall, without emitting a sound, tired. Nasula did not see or hear it.

'Catch it, there it is,' Sula said, halting in the doorway, panting and guarding the door in case the chicken tried to run out.

'Where?'

'There, behind the gourd.'

Nasula stood up and caught the chicken. Outside, using an old knife without a handle, she cut off the chicken's head and threw its body into a shallow tin by the doorside. Back inside, she replaced the knife where she had picked it from the roof of the hut and went and resumed sieving the cassava. Sula had already renewed her pounding.

The water started boiling. Nasula swooped the clay pot from the fire and poured the water into the shallow tin over the chicken. She called Sula over and they plucked the chicken, cut it into pieces and put it on the fire in a metallic pot.

The sky in the west was beginning to turn mauve from the impending twilight when they began completing the preparations of the cassava powder. It was then that a robust woman in a bright red *citenge* dress and red shoes, with a red belt tightly clasped around her waist and big, bouncy breasts tossing up and down as if she had eyes on them, appeared in the tiny, impoverished yard. The woman was carrying a baby in a sling on her back. Sula saw her first.

'Mother, there she is. That is the woman I was talking about,' she said, as she stopped scooping the pounded cassava out of the mortar.

Nasula turned round in the direction of the north path to the village and saw the familiar exuberant figure.

'That is Nalukwi,' she said, her heart dancing and a smile tugging at the corners of her mouth.

Nalukwi arrived in a burst of joy, the sheen of her body,

clothes and mood overwhelming the mother and her daughter. Nasula, up on her feet, was slapping the cassava powder dust off her dress, hair, face and arms, as she stepped backwards over the stool she had been sitting on, turned and took a couple of uneasy paces towards the newly arrived. Nalukwi, gay at every moment of her life, clucked happily, as she drew closer to Nasula and embraced her fondly.

Because Nalukwi had a baby on her back, Nasula could not wrap her arms around her older friend. She instead clasped her upper arms and, with their necks touching, the two women swayed like grass fronds in a breeze.

Sula swallowed understandingly before turning shyly away. Her mother did not usually display her feelings so openly.

'How long a time it has been, people; you are just well, Nasula of ours?' said Nalukwi when she and Nasula had parted and shaken hands in further happy greeting.

'It is enough that we can breathe and the sun rises and sets. What else can one expect from the life of today, Nalukwi of ours? But we are well, if everything is well where you have come from in the city?'

'The children and their father were well when I was leaving; hunger and suffering is the life of today.'

'A little breath, that is enough; what else can you say these days?'

'The days are bad – it is not a thing to say.'

'The gods alone know where things will end. You just wake up, watch the sun shining and then go back to sleep after another whole day of nothingness.'

Nasula looked around impatiently. Where was Sula to bring a stool? Sula was the word initiative. Before the mother could call her name and make this request, the girl came out of the kitchen carrying a three-legged carved stool, which she passed to the visitor after greeting her.

'This is Nalukwi, child, she is as good as my sister. You were a small thing when she and I were together in Lusaka,' Nasula said to Sula, looking at her daughter with a glow of affection. Turning to Nalukwi she continued: 'She says you recognised her when you saw her at the well this morning.'

'How could I not when she is you from toe to hair? What strong blood you have Nasula. Who would steal a child like this without being caught cheating? How the child has grown. How well behaved and intelligent she looks, *yantu yakwe Leza*! What do they say now, your in-laws?'

'What can they say? They are not the same people you know of. Have the child and I not just been talking about them? They have fallen and broken into pieces as a clay pot from the head of a tall woman.'

'Is it not said that the dead have eyes to see what the living are up to and able to punish their evil doing? I wish they were here, those Chiswebes. I would have sung *kakonko* for them and asked them to dance for me in broad daylight. Nasula, how those people danced on your head when you were mourning, a worse devil is yet to be born.'

'You wouldn't do it Nalukwi, with your good heart. It is a sad situation in which they are now. And Isaki has died.'

'You are talking, Nasula?'

'We buried him the day before yesterday.'

'And what may it be that ate him?' said Nalukwi gravely, looking startled. 'Let it not be, *iye*, this disease that has just come. Did I not hear he was a one who touched everywhere?'

'You have not said it, Nalukwi. It was a stick as thin as my finger that we buried. Was it Isaki Chiswebe, the Nsunzu mountain, which you saw at the funeral of the late in Lusaka?'

'These are bad years, Nasula,' Nalukwi said reminiscently, her voice low and plaintive. 'There is bitterness in the taste of life everywhere and in everything in the land. In the city and in

48

the village alike, the sun seems to be shining on nothing. It's a curse on us and on the land. You bring new people in government and hope the sky will open up and spill honey upon the earth; instead a dryness and a stubborn disease clothe it in harshness and blood.'

'Let us sit down.'

They sat down by the hut, to the right of the door, at a distance from the white cassava powder dust that arose when Sula started sieving the little pounded cassava remaining in the dish. How had Nalukwi travelled, Nasula enquired, and the other said she had travelled well and went on to give her friend more details about her journey and other little news about her life.

She had come to Wimbe her home village, Nalukwi said, a week ago to mourn her uncle, the elder brother of her mother, who had died a month ago of malaria, according to what people had told her. She would be going back to Lusaka on Thursday that week. She would leave from Wimbe on Wednesday for Senga Hill and jump on the bus to Lusaka on Thursday. She had come to Swelini yesterday and would be returning to Wimbe the following morning.

She had come to visit her in-laws, the family of Yowani Sikalumbi into which one of her brothers had married, to deliver a message from her brother and a gift – a small sewing machine.

By the way, in Lusaka, she and the family had moved from Chaisa compound five years previously and were now living in Mandevu, a large and more populated shanty compound full of the *Zezulu*. Damson Chipampe, her husband, was still languishing as a labourer and had recently been taken on by a company that was building new houses in Chilenje Township. You could not tell if he might stay in his new job this time. Work was difficult to keep these days, she would not be surprised if she found him already unemployed on her return.

49

She now had ten children, including the baby she was with. That was partly why they had shifted to Mandevu. The house they had been renting in Chaisa had become too small for the family, with seven children and six dependants. Damson Chipampe had had to look for a bigger house and he had found one in Mandevu. What could one do? These husbands of theirs who were not educated and thought only of beer and flesh were just another curse worse than a toothache. To them a woman's lot was just babies and more babies.

It was God who had caused her to meet the young one, Sula, at the well that morning, she said. Otherwise she would have gone back to Wimbe without seeing Nasula as the idea had not been in her head that Nasula could be living in Swelini. She had forgotten completely that Nasula had said she was of the village.

Nasula in turn confessed that she had forgotten that Nalukwi had once told her that she was of these parts of the land of the Lungu people of Mbala and had always imagined Nalukwi as being from somewhere further up, beyond the town of Mbala, near the Tanzanian border. Then she held the reins of the conversation and told Nalukwi of how she had returned to the village of Swelini and settled on that piece of land where they were now seated.

On arrival in the village, she said, she had gone straight to the home of the headman and explained her plight to him. He had shown her a hut within his compound for her to stay briefly while he consulted the village elders and decided on the piece of land on which she could settle down and build a home and grow her crops.

The place where they were now living was shown her after two weeks. In another two a hut was built for her by the young men and boys of the village, to whom she had paid money from the little change she had arrived with. She shifted to the hut as soon as it was completed and started her lonely struggle for survival, tilling the land in her own field and in those of other people. She worked in their fields and did other forms of piece work, such as cutting thatching grass for food, money, clothes and the other essentials of life. Often, due to pressure for what to eat and what to repay debts with, she had little time to work in her own field.

Her livelihood had therefore mainly depended on piece work. But during the nineties, especially of late, things had changed for the worse. The drought and the non-availability of fertilisers had complicated the livelihoods of many households. There was no money or produce to spare, and as a result, piece work had become very difficult to find; and unrewarding if and when you found it. Life was now a long hard struggle for survival.

Nasula's voice grew a note more plaintive with each word she uttered. A grievous colony of ants was eating at the stem of her soul, for she had the calamity of her daughter having to leave school at the centre of her mind.

The look on Nalukwi's face revealed that she had seen the dust-storm of pain in which her younger friend groped and she felt deeply for her. Suckling her baby and wriggling her bare toes, while she examined the shoe she had taken off, Nalukwi spoke, to save the other from the pain of further narrating her woes.

'That is the living of today,' she said soothingly. 'Ask me, Nasula of mine. Is everyone in the city not talking about wanting to leave the towns and come back to the village, thinking life is more endurable here in the rural areas? There is suffering in the city these days: so much you cannot say it, Nasula.'

'Hmm.'

There was something Nasula sensed in Nalukwi's eyes and in her voice, which stifled her speech to 'hmm'. Something similar to what she had felt at the sight and sound of the old man

Sikulukili Chiswebe a few days previously: the pain, pity and compassion for someone who had dwindled from robust life to a flicker of bare survival.

Nalukwi had suddenly become the oracle's mirror in which Nasula now stared at her own image. Was this the person Nalukwi now saw, someone ravaged by hardship? Had she dwindled to such a sorry state that she was responsible for the pity in Nalukwi's eyes and voice? She suddenly had an image of herself as someone in a permanent state of shrinking and losing colour, the way the old man Chiswebe had appeared to her as if he was slipping away and would eventually disappear into his dirty, crumpled black suit.

She was horrified. So horrified that she was left without words; so flooded by a feeling of despair that her heart cried out to Nalukwi.

'If I had a way, Nasula of mine, I would take you to Lusaka this moment for you to see how people are suffering in the city,' Nalukwi said. 'People are suffering in this our land. The city is worse because it even eats away at your dignity, which the village doesn't. New people are in the government and they appear to be changing things for a better today and tomorrow. There are no more shortages in the shops. But then there is no money with which to buy what you need.'

'And without money, where are you?'

'Are people in suits and ties, who look like ministers or even the president himself, not turning into cheats or outright thieves in order to survive?'

'What life is that?'

'They say the Lord Jesus Christ will come back to straighten things out on earth, but is he going to find anything left of this world by the time he comes? Is the world not ending just like this? Children as young as my Sula are becoming wells for every man on every street of the city – for money!'

'Sula, go into the hut and take a look in the pot that is on the fire,' Nasula said, inspecting her daughter's face for the effect of what Nalukwi had just said, but making nothing of the expression on the girl's face.

Sula disappeared into the hut, Nasula adjusted herself properly on the stool. Nalukwi's remarks occasioned an overgrowth of fresh thoughts about her quest for money with which to send Sula to school; these assailed her with the density and vigour of a jungle. In the grip of a consuming anxiety, she picked up the thread of the story of Sula's progress in school, their struggle and their failure to raise the one hundred thousand *kwacha* that was needed to send Sula to grade ten at St Theresa Girls Secondary School. Slowly but surely, she sewed the thread of memory from the beginning to the end. She ended at the point when she had sent Sula into the hut a while ago. Nalukwi was touched and she drew her bow like a miraculous huntswoman in a fairy tale.

'I heard you mention that you depend on the beans which you harvested in February for your relish and that you used them to exchange for cassava for *nshima*, and a few other things,' she said. 'How much of your bean harvest remains? Beans are very expensive in Lusaka at this time of the year, there are very few kinds available, especially the type that you grow here in Mbala, the yellow and white bean. Even if you have just one bag, it will give you the one hundred thousand *kwacha* that you need to send the child to school.'

'Are you talking, Nalukwi?' Nasula's eyes and mouth were suddenly wide with curiosity.

'A ninety k.g. bag of beans from here, is selling at one hundred and twenty thousand *kwacha* in Lusaka, now as I am talking to you. Do you think it's a lie that I am telling you?'

'Is it you Nalukwi talking?'

'If you can fill a bag with what has remained, we can go to

Lusaka together on Thursday. I say it to you, Nasula, you will be back here on Sunday with one hundred thousand *kwacha* and the child can go to her school in enough time, before the classes start.'

'Nalukwi, please don't kill me with something that might not be true. I am not myself here where I am sitting. I am trembling, I don't know why.'

'The child will go to school, Nasula; she must go, if there is a bag of beans to take her. A child like this is a future with which not everyone is blessed. The gods and the spirits will help you.'

'I pray to them all,' Nasula said, reverently, crossing her arms and resting her hands on her shoulders, as if Nalukwi herself were the gods and spirits before whom she sat for confession and salvation.

The young woman suddenly shuddered with expectation. The drought-ridden floor of her being lost its dry parchness, as if a soft rain had fallen bringing nourishment and vitality to the centre of her soul. She felt a fresh shoot of joyous hope spread reassuringly through her being.

Early in November the previous year, before planting maize, Nasula had planted two tins of yellow and white beans and harvested them in February. The crop had not been very good everywhere in the village but her own harvest had been reasonable. She had not measured what she had reaped, but to her eyes it was something that would give her and the child something to feed on for some time. Now it was May, three months after she had harvested the beans and started using them for relish and exchanging them for cassava for making *nshima*. She could not tell what quantity of the harvest she had used or what remained of it. She felt it was unlikely that she had used even half of her crop. She was sure, from intuition, that this was so. Whether or not the beans would make up a bag, she could not tell, but she had a feeling that a bag, just one bag, was something within reach.

'Sula, quick, my daughter,' she said, rising with a jerk. She had shouted, without knowing it.

Sula rushed out of the hut alarmed by the urgency in her mother's voice, blinking, her eyes tearful with the sting of smoke from the fireplace.

'Mother.'

'Be quick.'

'What is it, mother?'

'Go on asking questions if you don't want to go to school. Quick, my daughter, run to the home of Musalilwa and ask him to lend us his tin for measuring, so that we can see how many beans there are in the barn. Go immediately.'

'My father-in-law, Yowani Sikalumbi, has a tin too and a gallon drum,' Nalukwi said. 'Let her go there. It's nearer.'

'You hear, Sula, go instead to Yowani Sikalumbi's home and say Nalukwi has sent you for a tin and a gallon drum, and that Nalukwi will carry them back when she returns home later.'

When Sula returned with the tin and gallon drum, the two women and the girl went to the low, sagging barn with its rotting thatch, a little distance south of the hut. Together, they removed the beans from the barn and measured them. It came to one full bag, four tins, two gallons and a little more.

'There it is, Nasula,' Nalukwi said, standing back, the flats of her hands on the fronts of her thighs. 'What do you say?'

'Nalukwi, don't ask, we shall go to Lusaka together on Thursday,' replied Nasula stupefied with excitement. 'Transport money, how much could it be, the bag and the body?'

'Two tins will do at the price of beans by the roadside, at Senga Hill. Is it not two thousand five hundred *kwacha* per gallon?'

'Something like that.'

'You can sell two tins at Senga Hill and remain with two tins and two gallons for your food while the bag goes to Lusaka.'

'That is what we are going to do.'

'But mother, will two tins and two gallons be enough for food and . . .' Sula tried to interrupt, but was not given a chance.

'Keep quiet,' Nasula interrupted her; 'I will be alone and there will be a bit of maize a month from now. You must go to school!'

Sula looked at her mother, her gaze a mixture of awe and tenderness. Nasula's heart moved, she felt tears of hope and love for her daughter. She averted her head and fought her emotions away.

Her impending journey to Lusaka to sell the bag of beans occupied her mind again. She would have to find an empty grain bag in which to pack the beans, she thought, and a way of moving the beans to Senga Hill before Thursday. Where and how was she going to acquire an empty grain bag? How was she going to carry a bag and two tins of beans to Senga Hill? Would she be able to sell two tins to raise money for her transport to Lusaka? Would she be able to load the remaining beans on to the vehicle?

'Friends, let us cook and eat supper, I must go out and start looking for an empty grain bag to put the beans in and young men in the village to help me carry the beans to Senga Hill for a payment within my reach.'

'I have grain bags in Wimbe,' Nalukwi said. 'I will give you one big one, the ninety k.g., and two fifty k.g. ones, the new ones the new government has introduced. One of my brothers will be escorting me to Senga Hill with a bicycle. I will talk to him and two of my sisters to help us carry the beans on Wednesday. The one with the bicycle can carry the ninety k.g. bag, we can carry one tin each, and share the travelling bags between us.'

A silence of shocked appreciation followed. The silence swallowed Nalukwi in its warmth and appreciation. It haunted the trio through to the supper of *nshima* with chicken cooked in honour of Nalukwi. Afterwards, while Nasula and her daughter were seeing off the visitor, it was agreed that Nasula would go with Nalukwi the following morning to Wimbe village to collect the empty grain bags, and confirm the arrangements with her family.

The sun had long set and it was very dark.

◆

Wimbe was to the east and a few hours' walking distance from Swelini. Nasula went there and back on the same day. Nalukwi was someone who was very much respected in her family. Everything happened and was agreed upon according to her word. On Tuesday, when it was dark, Nasula changed into a *citenge*, which she wrapped tightly round her waist; then she washed her dress and dried it over the fire. Nalukwi had given her a bit of washing powder, and a little Vaseline jelly to apply to her body. In the morning, before sunrise, Nalukwi and her brother and sisters arrived from Wimbe ready for the journey to Senga Hill.

Part Two

What powers of darkness

Chapter Four

Without lightning or thunder

Arrival is the birth of a new life. The newly arrived must brace for things good as well as strange and poisonous. Prayer is called for. The newly arrived must spread their souls before the gods and beg for the power to live as the spirit longs to. To defeat the strange and poisonous is a difficult thing on one's own. Without the light and breath of the gods, one cannot be sure of victory.

Nasula summoned the gods in silence. She prayed to be kept safe from marauding thieves at the market place.

The woman's thoughts were infested with the wasps and stings of fear. Her bag of beans was the last piece of firewood at the hearth of her desire to send Sula to secondary school. The bag must not go missing. There would be no tomorrow for her daughter if the bag was stolen. The relief of reaching a desired destination must not blind her to danger. She must be wise and watch out for any ominous signs.

The truck that had brought her to Lusaka stood still and majestic like a zebra tamed into a transport animal, facing the deep orange fireball of the setting sun. Kamwala market was closed and deserted for the day, except for the traders from distant places who slept there. It lay sprawled in a drab mass of stalls constructed from wood, cardboard, plastic, bricks and scrap metal. Standing over everything was a concrete block and steel structure, the main market building.

The city centre lay to the north west, immersed in the shadows of twilight. A faint breeze whispered through the air above the drone of vehicles.

With her back to the cabin of the truck, the woman stood leaning against the steel bars that were welded on to the edge of the carrier. She was standing next to her bag of beans, a little apart from the few remaining passengers, watching carefully. She was a patient owl, full of apprehension and mistrust of the world before her.

As soon as the truck had pulled into the market, a swarm of suspicious-looking young men emerged from nowhere. They sallied forth in all directions, screaming and whistling in jubilation. Without asking, some of them jumped on to the truck and busied themselves passing the luggage down to their friends below who were simultaneously shouting and shoving everybody around. They claimed to want to help with the offloading, so that the owners would give them some money.

What madness! Was that the way to help or acquire a job? The woman jerked upright and began guarding her beans to prevent the bag being moved by anybody, watching with petrified keenness the luggage being removed from the truck. She had done this on the way as well. Whenever the truck had stopped to pick up or drop someone, she had risen and watched the movements of both the people and the luggage, making sure nothing happened to her bag of beans. Now, at this last moment of her journey, she was even more concerned. Summoning the power of the gods, she waited intently for the commotion to die down, before she risked taking her bag out of the truck.

The commotion around the truck was murderous. The vehicle was big and had picked up a lot of people and luggage on the way. Men and women of peasant stock carrying different produce for sale in the city: groundnuts, millet, sorghum, sweet potatoes and vegetables. Due to the raucous interference of the young men and their uninvited invasion of the truck, everyone felt their produce was in jeopardy.

Somewhere in the distance, a train moaned like a beast of

prey, followed by the heavy metallic sound of wagons ramming into each other and the clang of rolling steel. On the truck, a man's rough voice hollered at an unwanted helper, commanding the culprit not to be a fool and touch any of his bags. His target ignored the order and made to lift the bag of sorghum in front of him, saying he would not ask for a large payment, just something small, enough to buy a cup of tea. The man who had shouted called him the son of a dog and pushed him roughly away, so that he fell back on his haunches.

'Why are you villagers so stingy with your money?' the discarded samaritan complained forlornly, thrusting himself to his feet with an air of self-righteousness as if the bag's owner had no right to do what he had done. He was a good-looking young man, almost a boy, with an intelligent face and thoughtful eyes, an initiate in the lost world of the city.

'Away from here!'

'What do you think others will eat if you are so mean when times are so hard?'

'Who tells you that I have any money on me?' the villager retaliated forcefully.

'You can just give me a bit of your produce and let me sell it myself or exchange it for something else.'

'My friend, I am tired, leave me in peace; you have no idea where I am coming from and how I have moved.'

Below, in the direction of the market, a woman implored another to stop what she was doing and give the baby her breast – the baby was stabbing at her soul with its hungry, imploring cries. A man cursed and complained that someone had poured water on his bag of groundnuts. The woman with the crying baby sat down on a bundle of clothing and started feeding her child, while the man whose groundnuts had been soaked with water paced about in frustrated anger, unable to tell who the culprit was.

63

All this and a lot more, the woman observed in silence, her mind wrapped round the precious treasure, her bag of mixed yellow and white beans.

'Nasula,' the familiar motherly voice of Nalukwi called out. Such was her preoccupation that she had forgotten all about Nalukwi. She only remembered as she heard her voice. 'Nasula, where are you? What are you doing? Nasula, I am here.'

Nalukwi had already alighted from the truck and taken down her luggage, a medium-sized travelling bag made from a black plastic material which she had placed firmly beside her on the dusty ground of the market place.

'Eh-he, you are down already?' Nasula said, shaking off the slumber of her concentration. 'I see you are there, Nalukwi.'

'What are you doing? Ask someone to help you move the bag near the edge and I will lift it down here; these women will help me.'

'Wait a little,' responded Nasula looking from Nalukwi down to her bag and back; 'let the ones with much luggage and those who are in a hurry clear theirs first.'

'The time, Nasula, it will soon be dark. We must find a good place in the market for you to spend the night. Now. Before it gets dark. We need to move fast.'

'Wait just a little.'

An infant wailed thirstily on a mother's back. It was Nalukwi's baby. Nasula found a better excuse.

'The baby, Nalukwi, feed the baby first,' she said.

With swift hands, Nalukwi shifted the baby from her back to her chest without having to untie the *citenge* in which the child was being carried. Hushing and shaking her last-born, she sat down on her bag, tossed out a breast from under her dress and started suckling the baby. Nasula put her foot on her bag of beans and continued watching the other passengers off-loading their luggage and alighting from the truck.

Nalukwi stopped feeding the baby and threw it back on her back. The commotion had more than halved. The truck was almost empty. Nasula tightened the *citenge* her friend had lent her, to shield herself from the wind and cold, and checked the position of her sackcloth bag hanging from her right shoulder. When Nalukwi started moving towards the truck, she bent down and clasped each horn of her bag of beans. Alone, she pulled the bag along the floor of the truck's carrier and leaned it against the vehicle's right side. A male and female passenger came over and offered a hand. With their help, she lifted the bag and lowered it down the side of the truck to Nalukwi and three other women from whom Nalukwi had requested assistance. Then, quickly, she climbed down out of the truck using one of its rear tyres as her ladder.

The place where produce such as beans, groundnuts, millet and sorghum were displayed for selling in bulk, at the Kamwala market, was at the south-western end. It was an open space bordered on the east and north by stalls.

While Nasula looked after the baggage, Nalukwi found a place along the eastern line of market stalls for Nasula to store her bag of beans and sleep.

It was a narrow piece of dry ground between two wooden stands. The plastic papers with which the roof of each stall was covered, met in such a way that the two roofs had become one, so that Nasula and her bag of beans would not get soaked even if it rained. So, there was no need to negotiate for a place with those who had tents or sheds who would mostly likely ask for payment. These were the nineties. Nothing was offered for nothing.

'The place is something,' Nalukwi said when they had put the bag down and positioned it well, and the women who had helped them lift the bag had gone away, leaving the two of them alone. 'One day cannot make an elephant rotten.'

'What is important is that we've arrived safely; and without anything crossing the path ahead of us as a bad omen.'

'The spirits have blessed us.'

'It is a thing to be thankful for.'

They were standing beside each other and in front of the bag of beans, scruffy and worn after the long journey. They had not been able to take the bus on Thursday, as they had thought they would. It had not been possible because of the beans. The driver and bus conductor had said there was no space for the bag in the bus. They had instead taken their chance on a truck at first cockcrow that Friday morning. The journey had thus taken longer, and had been less comfortable, than it would have been in a bus.

'Let me bring you something to sleep on and cover yourself with,' Nalukwi said and hurried away to where she had left her own bag. She returned a little while later and gave Nasula a blanket and a sheet from her bag. After that, she went away again and came back with a bunch of torn paper sacks, once used to hold concrete, which she gave to Nasula and told her to use them to cover the ground, before she slept.

A man was passing by at a distance, sauntering in a northerly direction. He was in late middle age, long-haired and stooped, with a high forehead and bushy eyebrows that gave him an air of gravitas, given to the harsh practicalities of life rather than unnecessary chatter. He wore an old-fashioned dark suit that looked heavy on him and was creased and torn in places. Seeing him, Nalukwi stared at the man thoughtfully and then greeted him.

'Is that greeting meant for me?' the man said in a deep, pleasant voice, stopping and staring in the direction from which it had come from.

'How are you?'

'I am well, if you are well too?' the man said in a fatherly way and came over to where Nalukwi and Nasula were standing beside each other, facing the man, the bag of beans behind them.

'I thought I could find out something from you,' Nalukwi said to the stranger, shifting her baby from her front to her back. 'They say if you ask, you will not swallow what is poisonous and die from eating something others know is not good for eating.'

'They also say wisdom comes from asking and they are not wrong. A person cannot be aware of every secret in the world.'

'You have been here for some days? I see as if you are the owner of the beans under that green tent near the road.'

'Those are my beans. I am two days here.'

'It is the price of beans that I am trying to discover,' Nalukwi said. 'What is the price that everybody is selling at?'

'One hundred thousand to one hundred and twenty thousand *kwacha* for a ninety k.g. bag, depending on the type of beans you have to sell,' the man explained. 'My beans are the brown ones from Solwezi; I am selling them at a hundred flat.'

'Our beans are the yellow and white ones from Mbala.'

'Ah!' the man exclaimed. 'They are diamonds, don't haggle. They will go at one hundred and twenty thousand *kwacha*. No one has them here. How many bags do you have with you?'

'This one only.'

'It's nothing, they will be bought first thing in the morning. They will be gone before ten.'

Nasula's heart danced with elation. A soft breeze of hope and pleasure swept through her and she thought fondly about Nalukwi. She was a dependable spirit. She had not lied or dreamt of the impossible. Beans were medicine here in the city at this time of the year. This one bag of beans alone, would fetch her, Nasula, the money she needed to send her daughter to school and allow a balance of twenty thousand *kwacha* for her travel back home. Nalukwi was an oracle, a miracle.

After further conversation, the man from Solwezi said good evening and left. Nalukwi turned to Nasula with a look of contented reassurance.

'It will be all right, things will go well,' she said. 'Beans have always been precious during this time, especially the ones from our parts.'

'A big blessing it will surely be.'

'You will sell the bag and buy what you have to buy before noon. You can spend the afternoon resting at my home and leave on Sunday.'

'If things go well that early.'

'I will come here in the morning to be with you and help where necessary. It's becoming dark. Let me leave you to rest. It is also far where I have to go and catch a minibus to Mandevu. The station is the other side of town. But what are you going to eat, Nasula of ours?'

'Some groundnuts remained, it shouldn't worry you. I am not that hungry.'

'You will have a good meal tomorrow, the spirits have already seen us to the place where we wanted to be.'

'Don't say it, Nalukwi. You don't know it yourself. It is a big thing you have done to make me come here with this bag of beans. I will never find words for you.'

The gaze of the two met and interlocked. A moment passed. Nasula felt her eyes held by the kindness in the glow of the older woman's look. A soothing warmth seemed to flow from her eyes.

'Greet everybody at home.'

'Remain well.'

They shook hands and said goodnight. Nalukwi lifted her bag to her head. Looking forward with keen anticipation to tomorrow's promised conclusion of the purpose of her journey to Lusaka, Nasula watched Nalukwi disappear behind the clusters of empty stalls in the gathering dusk.

She could not remember when the white and black truck on which they had journeyed had driven off. But the truck was no longer there. The commotion was over. Only a spell of tired quietness and speculation hung upon the market like a low, harmless cloud above a forest.

The space between the bag of beans and the stand on the northern side was just large enough for one person to sleep. Nasula took better inspection of the place now that she was alone and decided that she was going to sleep with her head towards the east. Savouring her decision, she sat down on the bottom end of the bag, facing the horizon where the sun had disappeared, her heart a shimmering coal of joy and expectation.

The blanket and sheet Nalukwi had given her to use for the night lay on the upper end of the bag behind her. Without looking backwards, she drew them towards her, and lifting them to her lap, began to admire them. She had not slept or covered herself with such good bedding for many years. Smelling them, feeling and imagining her daughter at St Theresa Secondary School, she decided that she would buy Sula such a blanket and bedsheet.

She would do it, she thought. Was it not only after one single night that she would possess the most money she had ever had? Sula had grown into a big girl and was going into grade ten. The child could not continue sleeping on empty sacks and bare reed mats while covering herself with a torn second-hand *citenge*. The child should have better things to sleep on and cover herself with. Come tomorrow, she would buy Sula a blanket and bedsheet that were new, straight from where they had been made, and as good as the ones on her lap which Nalukwi had left her to use for the night.

Slowly, the feel of the blanket dissolved into a dream. She saw Sula in a white suit walking down Cairo Road, her head held high, her step firm, her direction independent. She, a poor miserable woman of the village was the mother of the *namukokolo*, one that would rise high. She saw herself fall on her knees in thanksgiving.

The dream wore off and she descended back into the real world and discovered that she was dozing as she sat on her bag of beans, holding the blanket and bedsheet that Nalukwi had left her. The twilight had been eaten by night and everywhere on the horizon, the blanket of darkness was punctuated by the sharp glow of electric light.

Tiredness tore at her muscles with violence. She felt like sleeping but the rumbling of hunger in the pit of her stomach gnawed her awake. She took out some crumbs of cassava and a handful of groundnuts from her sackcloth bag and ate them for her supper.

After that, she stood up and, stretching herself, she gathered up the thick torn paper sacks and covered the ground between the bag and the stand on the northern side. She next spread her *citenge* over the papers and lay down, covering herself with the bedsheet and blanket.

Chapter 5

Black daylight

She woke up several times during the night, afraid of over-sleeping. The sound of moving vehicles began. She woke up for good. It was before six. Through the openings between the timber off-cuts with which the stands were built, day had hardly begun to break.

Yawning, stretching herself, she slid her feet into her tropical sandals, stood up and untied the kerchief from her head. Holding one corner in each of her hands, she waved it up and down, careful the aged cloth did not give way and tear in more places than it had already done. Satisfied she had dusted and straightened the kerchief enough, she folded it carefully so that the folds hid most of the torn or dirty patches. Then she tied it round her head, covering her hair completely so that nothing unkempt was betrayed to the world.

She picked up the *citenge*, which had acted as a cover, dusted it and then tied it round her waist. After this she folded the blanket and the bedsheet and carefully put them aside on a piece of paper by the stand on the northern side. Thinking of what else she should do, she concluded there was nothing more for the time being and sat down on the bag of beans.

She felt cold. She unfolded the blanket and covered herself with it from shoulder to shin. Thus she waited for the day to break, thinking about her daughter.

Sula, her daughter, was a blessing. She took her schooling seriously and had refused to be weighed down by the severity of their poverty or the reality that she had no father, and that she was a girl, not a boy. Given support, she would become success-

71

ful and be able to make decisions about her own life, she would make them achieve as a family. The child was a cowrie of hope. A great gift from the gods to one who was so poor and lowly, to wear round one's neck for inspiration, and, above all, hope.

The day Sula had started going to school, Nasula had folded her hands and prepared herself for the many problems, the nagging demands that she had heard other parents complain they received from their school-going children. There were stories about pupils not wanting to go to school wearing the same clothes, or carrying the same food, too often, especially if their clothes or food shamed them or made them the butt of scornful laughter. There were also stories about poor school performance, and bad conduct, such as stealing and fighting, by certain pupils.

Nasula had worried herself sick – she had severe headaches – about how to make her daughter understand why her mother could not, for example, buy her shoes or a satchel. How was she going to survive the torture of such incidents and maintain her daughter's interest in going to school?

She was further terrified at the thought of what she would do if Sula turned out to be a difficult child who did not behave well in class. How was she going to bring Sula back to the right path without causing her harm and without being accused by teachers or onlookers of being a complacent mother, or, worse still, one who was a bad influence on her daughter? It would be a painful problem to solve; for Sula was not just any child to treat with firmness. Sula belonged to the wretched of the earth, she was one of the ill-fated seedlings of the world, sown at the edge of the cliff of darkness.

Sula was a child who had lost a father. Fatherless she was living in poverty with a mother without means or relatives to lean on. Maybe the world saw nothing unusual in all this. But to Nasula, a mother, Sula was different. She was no ordinary

72

child. Even when at her happiest, she still looked solitary as if her mind was preoccupied elsewhere.

The child required a delicate hand to guide her from the cliff, on which the death of her father had left her balancing precariously, down to the valley of light and hope below. How was she, Nasula, going to succeed in guiding the little one down to the valley of life, without tripping the child over the cliff? How was she going to manage to straighten the seedling without snapping its delicate stem?

But seven years had passed and her daughter had completed her primary school education without one problem coming Nasula's way. Throughout all those years of the child's school life, Nasula had known only peace, and received only praise for her daughter's performance at school.

Unlike other children in Swelini and the surrounding villages, Sula, from the first day, never complained about what she wore or took to school. She had never demanded anything. When something was needed at school and the teachers told the pupils to ask their parents for it, Sula would not do so. Only sometimes would she inform her mother that such a thing was needed at school. She always deliberately avoided saying that the teachers had told the pupils that their parents must provide them with the item. Nor had she ever threatened not to go to school or stop schooling if such or such happened or didn't happen.

Soon after she had begun school, word started coming home that she was an intelligent, determined girl who did not miss classes, was interested in learning, and punctual. That she was not discouraged or forced into fighting, at what the other pupils said and did to her, because of the poverty of her clothing, school bag and the food she took with her.

Sula's school bag, for example, was a gaudy affair made of old, different coloured materials which Nasula had sewn together in desperation and it was the source of much laughter and scorn. But Sula still carried the bag with amazing confidence and pride – and in patch-ridden, threadbare clothes without shoes on her feet.

The laughter, jokes, teasing and other aggressive group behaviour fell on deaf ears and never made the girl cry or become angry as would have been expected. People saw this and were struck with admiration. So they talked about the legend and brought word to Nasula, the lucky mother of such a child.

The first time Nasula was told about how other children teased her daughter and how her daughter ignored them and held her head high, the story so touched her that when those who had relayed the story had gone and she was alone, she broke down and wept. She was moved to tears because Sula herself had never mentioned this ordeal.

All along, Nasula had feared that her daughter might be laughed at, given the child's awkward clothes and possessions. The possibility haunted her and made her wonder how she would pacify and comfort the little one. But she had deceived herself. She thought that when something of this nature occurred, she would either hear about it from her daughter's mouth or see it on her daughter's face.

But what she feared had already occurred and done so without her hearing a thing from Sula or noticing anything herself. She had remained in the dark until she had been told by other people.

She was quiet about it, but not for long. The day came and she talked. She could not hold words to herself for more than a few days. They were at the stream, alone, the two of them as usual, sitting on their haunches opposite each other, removing soaked tubers of cassava from a nearby pool and peeling the tubers ready for pulverising and drying.

'Someone told me your friends at school laugh at you because of what you wear and carry to school. Is this true?' she said, and pretended to be looking into the pool while she watched Sula so anxiously out of the corner of her eye, that she was afraid she might shed tears the moment the child opened her mouth.

'There are few remaining,' the girl said staring into the water to take a good look at the cassava tubers that were still there. 'One. Perhaps two.'

'Did you hear my question?'

'Ah, mother, you ask about pupils at our school?' Sula said, laughing and clapping her hands, with gestures almost like an adult. '*Iyee!* They can make you cry, mother, if you are not serious. They are the ones who will laugh at anything, fight over nothing and cry anyhow.'

'*Ala?*'

'*Iye mwe!*'

'It is good you, my child, are not like them.'

'They laugh at me and joke about my clothes, my school bag and other things, even my food. But I don't cry or try to fight anyone.'

'Those are the ways of a good child.'

'Now, look at them when we are in class; would you say they are the ones, mother?' Sula said. She laughed and clapped her hands again. 'Most of them don't answer a single question from the teachers; they won't even open their mouths to try and give the correct answer. Mother, you can laugh. But I don't laugh at any of them.'

'That is good.'

'But they? *Iyee mwee!* When the one who is teaching goes and before the next one comes, they taunt each other about whatever little thing happened in the last class. Then they insult each other, fight and cry.'

'What children!'

'Mother, *ala* you can get annoyed and laugh at the same time.

What a noise they make when there isn't a teacher in the classroom or when one is there but concentrating on something else. The teachers ask them why they cannot be like me. They don't listen. They just want to laugh at me: my clothes, my things. But I always remember what you told me the night before I went to school. You told me that I should only worry about my lessons and nothing else; that I should think of where I come from, and remember that we are poor people with no one to turn to. So I just look at them and try to learn.'

Sadness, like dust, settled inside Nasula. The innocent wisdom, maturity and spirit of the child took her aback. Talking to her daughter was talking to a spirit. She should not have started the discussion, she thought, fighting back the tears welling in her eyes.

The girl herself seemed to have been taken over by a spirit. She fell quiet and showed no intention of saying another word, as if she was aware that if she said another word she would make her mother cry.

'You should tell me some of these things yourself; I shouldn't hear about them from other people first,' Nasula decided to end the conversation. 'I am your mother and a mother is the one to whom you should tell such things,' she said as firmly as she could. Then she continued, 'Let us quicken up and finish what we are doing.'

Sula barely nodded and continued working quietly, looking only at the cassava root she was peeling. Nothing was said between mother and daughter until they finished peeling the roots and went home, balancing the round reed baskets dripping with water from the cassavas, which were still wet, on their heads.

Soon after the next term started, Sula, as if prompted by their discussion, began showing her mother her written exercises and the comments the teachers had made against her work. Because her mother could not read nor write, Sula read and explained these to her.

The remarks were always very good, right up to the senior years of her primary schooling. Her position in class never went below fourth. In her last year, she came first in both the first and second terms. In the final examinations, she did so well that her result was the best in the school. She was one of only four pupils who made it to secondary school.

Nasula's memories enlivened her. Thoughts that held a tang of life and death suspended in the cadences of new morning. She could not help but feel impatient for daylight and the commencement of buying and selling at the market.

Time moved slowly. The first fingers of the sun streaked the eastern sky a pale mauve. Day was breaking. Nasula rose, removing the blanket from around her shoulders and body, folded it and put it back with the bedsheet, on the rough papers by the stand on the northern side.

The two stands between which she had slept faced east away from the open space where produce was sold in bulk, which was to the west. A few steps directly behind the stand on the northern side, stood a scarred mulberry tree with many branches. She went to the tree and snapped off a fresh twig about the length and thickness of a finger. After peeling one end of the stick, she chewed the end into a brush and started cleaning her teeth.

The sun finally rose and began its ascent into the limpid sky in a reddish orange glow. Streams of humanity laden with merchandise emerged in all directions. Vans, trucks, cars, wheelbarrows, bicycles and all manner of other transport carrying items for sale, people coming to do business: men, women, boys, girls and small children could be seen everywhere off-loading goods, counting out and displaying things for sale, writing and reading out figures. Kamwala market quickly turned into a mound inhabited by a huge, hungry tribe of termites in search of a livelihood.

A termite mound of many soils: grain, spare parts, vegetables, *salaula*, fresh and dried fish, *kapenta*, groceries, furniture, traditional medicines, new clothing, and so on. The eye could not pick out and digest everything. Many and good soils. The lack of variety, the poverty of the soils they had grown used to before the nineties, were not in sight. The nineties had become, as Nalukwi had truly said during their conversation in the village, years of no money but plenty to sell. The nineties were years of sale, not purchase.

Nasula took her time cleaning her teeth with the mulberry stick. She told herself not to get excited and hurry into displaying her bag of beans when there were no likely buyers in sight. She would display her bag later.

She went on, cleaning her teeth, pacing about beside her bag of beans and watching others busy at work, as if she had nothing to sell herself.

In the open space before her, where beans and other produce was sold in bulk, people assiduously occupied themselves standing their bags in the best positions, adjusting them for improvement, opening bags so the goods could be easily seen and felt by the buyers. Some arranged the bags in straight lines, some in circles and others in heaps. Everybody was trying to gain some advantage over their competitors.

Beyond the market, the swarms of humanity plodding to their offices and work places grew thicker and more confused with each blink of the eye. The modern metal lions, tigers, elephants, duikers, impalas, beetles and other breeds of transport multiplied their broods on the roads with each intake of breath, the noise they produced growing into a thunderous roar like a waterfall and drowning the serenity of the morning.

Almost at the same time, the owners of the stands between which she had slept, arrived and there was activity on and outside their stalls. She became uneasy standing between them. So she threw away the mulberry stick with which she had been cleaning her teeth, tightened the *citenge* briskly round her waist, held the bag of beans by its horns, and without help from anybody, pulled it to a place directly west of the mulberry tree.

On hard, parched ground lightly covered with grains of sand, she leaned her bag of beans against a stone, opening it just enough for a hand of any size to scoop a few beans, sift them through thoughtful fingers, and drop them back without anything having been spilled.

After she had done this, she went back to the place where she had slept and picked up the blanket, bedsheet and her bag of sackcloth. These she put under the mulberry tree. Then she stood between the tree and the bag of beans facing south so that she could keep an eye on both her beans and her possessions.

The first person to stop by her bag of beans was a busy-looking young woman in a dark suit who looked as if she worked in good offices. She asked the price and was told one hundred and twenty thousand *kwacha*. The woman then wrote something down on a piece of paper and walked quickly but gracefully away.

The second potential buyer came a while later. She was a fat, talkative woman with a dark, rough skin and long greying hair combed backwards and tied behind her head with a piece of cloth the same colour as that of the green *citenge* in which she was tightly clothed. So tightly clothed from shoulder to ankle, that her breasts and bottom rocked with every step she made.

'These are beans from Mbala District,' she said, passing a finger through the legumes. 'You can't tell me not.'

'They are from there.'

'Let me hear a good price from you and this bag is mine. The money is here.'

She patted the portion of her waist above her left hip to indicate where she kept her money. Nasula laughed shyly, telling herself that she had received one who was another one.

'Don't laugh, good one, you are a mother like me. Money has become difficult to find. The new people in government are closing state companies east, west, north and south. The result: all men in the country have lost their jobs and become hopeless. They spend time begging for beer in the bars to drown their sorrows instead of looking for food for their children to eat. The mother is the one who feels the pain of a new life coming into the world. She must fight on, alone, for something that her children can swallow. A mother cannot fail to understand the pain and suffering of another mother. Is that a lie?'

'It is not a lie.'

'Must not a mother then give another mother a price that is of the church? Go on, good one, what are you giving these beans to me for?'

'One twenty only.'

'Go away from here,' cried the fat woman, throwing a dismissive hand into the air. 'Friend, when did you last go to church? I can afford eighty.'

'We have a problem then.'

'Why, good one?'

'It cannot work.'

'Nothing fails to work between mothers. If you are so hard-hearted, I can add another ten. But I will go back home without a loaf of bread and a packet of sugar for the children's breakfast.'

'Anything less than one twenty will not work.'

The fat woman, talking with fast extravagance, tried again but she failed to bend Nasula. She left, promising to return when she had raised a hundred thousand *kwacha*. As soon as she was gone the man from Solwezi, whom Nalukwi had spoken to previously, about the price of beans, came and greeted Nasula.

'Serious buyers have not started arriving yet,' he said conversationally. 'It is still early. What was that woman who has just gone saying?'

Nasula explained.

'Don't waste your time with her if she comes again,' the man said. 'She sells beans at this market, in the vegetable section. She and others of that section sell beans and other things in small quantities packed in plastic bags. When they see someone new, like you, they try to force you into selling your produce at their price, so that they can gain more when they resell. These beans will not go for anything less than one twenty.'

'I'll not listen to her.'

'They are not people to deal with,' the man said. 'They make a lot of money even when they buy at the normal price, but they still want to steal more from you.'

Seeing a couple arrive to look at his beans, the man excused himself and rushed off.

More people came and went, appreciating the beans as being good, but not buying the bag. Some blamed their failure to do this on the price, others on the government which they said had made money difficult to find. Yet others gave no excuses and went away silently, as if for them nothing in the world was right or wrong.

The day had come of age. The shops and offices had opened and there were people at the market who went beyond asking the prices of produce and did their buying. The sky was clear like natural water, the sun whitish gold, fiercely bright and hot. Nasula wanted to sit down under the mulberry tree – she was beginning to feel hot, bored and tired – when an odd-looking, middle-aged woman of medium build and gnarled hands that

81

seemed to twitch, as if from need of alcohol, stormed towards Nasula's bag of beans.

'This is what I am looking for,' the woman said excitedly. 'These are the beans. How much are you selling the bag for?'

'One twenty.'

'I have no quarrel with your price but let me give you a hundred, that is what I have.'

'Add twenty thousand.'

At that very moment a man with a Homburg, which added to his stature, and a scent which smelt, if not expensive, then not natural, loomed before the two women, drawing them into the glow of his presence, and interrupting what Nasula had been about to say. Well built and in his late thirties, the man had well-cropped brown hair, a scanty brown beard and broad shoulders. He wore an immaculate checked suit, dark shoes, a white shirt and a red tie.

Although there was something shrewd, and not transparent, about his long, scar-marked face and bright eyes, the man was impressive taken altogether; and the gaiety of his disposition was charming to the eye and mind.

'I'll give you one hundred and thirty thousand *kwacha, mama,* for this bag,' he said. 'These are good beans.' His polished accent and the rather scented odour of his body, seemed to intimidate Nasula. 'What do you say, *mama*?'

She looked at the woman who had offered her a hundred thousand *kwacha*, as if to ask if she could afford the additional thirty thousand *kwacha* the man had offered. The other pouted her lips and bent her head to one side indicating defeat. Nasula shrugged and looked down at her bag of beans which was now about to leave her, a breeze of relief and happiness rising inside her heart.

'Did you say one thirty?' she asked the man, to be sure she had heard him correctly.

'Correct, *mama*.'

'You can take the bag.'

'Close it up, *mama*, I will find some boys to come and lift it into the car for me.'

The woman who had offered a hundred thousand *kwacha* and the man who had offered more, left in opposite directions, like enemies who did not want to go the same way after the war.

Nasula started sewing up the opening to the bag. As she finished, the man who had offered to buy the bag arrived with three young men and asked them to lift the bag into his car. The young men dropped the bag into a horizontal position. One of them held the horns while each of the other two grasped one of the two bottom corners. Nasula stepped forward to help the young man at the front. Then they all lifted the bag to the car with the man who was buying the beans striding ahead of them.

The car was parked by the edge of the market, along the road that marked the southern border. It was a bright yellow car with a black line on its sides. A beautiful machine, as immaculate as its owner. Nasula's eyes darted from one to the other, as the man opened his boot and she and the helpers threw her bag of beans inside.

When he had closed and locked the boot, the man who was buying the bag of beans fished out a five hundred *kwacha* note and gave it to the oldest of the three young men, saying that he and his friends would know how to share the money.

'Come, *mama*, let us go,' he said to Nasula and started walking back in the direction from which they had come. 'I want to buy some more of these beans.'

Still walking, he took out a bunch of notes and counted them, making Nasula's heart throb with anxiety.

'Six hundred thousand *kwacha*, I must buy three more bags and hire a van to take them home,' he said to himself, loudly enough for Nasula to hear. But then he did not give Nasula her share of his wealth. He put everything back in his pocket and walked on.

Reaching the spot where Nasula had been selling the beans, he told her to wait there a bit longer.

'Let me see if I can find some more beans like yours,' he said walking northwards towards another part of the market.

Nasula waited and waited and the man did not come. She became impatient and decided to follow him. She followed the passage along which he had walked, there was no sign of him. She walked down every passage where produce was sold in bulk, searching for him, but in vain. She decided to go and wait for him by his car. The yellow car had gone.

The nearby vendors confirmed her fears. It was clear that the man had cheated her out of her bag of beans.

Chapter Six

Echoes of darkness

Suffering woman, what is it that you have done to deserve this misfortune? What trouble have you caused against the gods? What have you spat on the shrine of your ancestors? A soul cannot be condemned to misfortune forever. This is too much.

She did not cry along with her thoughts sitting hunched on the folded bedsheet and blanket under the mulberry tree, waiting for Nalukwi to come to the market, the side of her head resting on her knees, her arms wrapped round her legs. The shock was far too deep.

Everything about her seemed to fall into oblivion. There was a semblance of peace, clarity and orderliness, now that she had been left alone, forgotten by the world. The existence in which the people at the market had immersed her, following the discovery of the theft, had been chaotic. Soon after the story of her loss had spread, she had been surrounded by a large crowd of strangers wanting to hear from her mouth exactly what had happened.

Men and women, girls and boys, children. They watched her like a lost pet, asking her questions. Even questions unrelated to her loss. What tribe was she? Had she a husband and children? Did she go to church? *Iye kalanda we!* Like a poisoned fish, confused and frightened, she gasped out the story before an ever thickening and jostling throng. They listened, and shook their heads in disbelief, resignation, or amused recognition at what people in the capital city were capable of doing; blending sadness and laughter into one fruit for the consumption of they knew better what spirits.

With time, an eternity of time, the commotion died down and the crowd melted away leaving her alone. That was when she sat down on the bedding under the mulberry tree and now, apart from the semblance of peace, clarity and orderliness, she felt the growing heaviness of her soul and spirits. The sun was still very hot and bright but she did not bother to move into the shadow of the mulberry tree. She continued sitting on the other, opposite, side, outside and a distance away from the shadow.

A familiar voice, full of life, suddenly called her name. She looked up and saw Nalukwi coming towards her. Emotion surged through her. She bit her lips in a bid to keep herself collected before the one who had done so much for her, and whose goodness always occasioned a swelling of emotions.

But when Nalukwi arrived, her voice and her presence so stirred Nasula's feelings that instead of a calm response, she just looked at her friend, and did not reply to her greeting; the expression on her face so flat that Nalukwi's own became a shroud of curiosity.

'Nasula, has something bad happened to you?' Nalukwi said, her face strained with anxiety. 'What is wrong?'

She tightened the *citenge* in which she was carrying the baby and bent forward towards Nasula, resting her hands on her knees.

'Something bad has happened, Nasula?'

Nasula nodded. Tears pricked her eyes and she wept. She wept only once and stopped, shrugging herself out of self-pity.

'How are the children and their father at home?' she said, rubbing the tears from her face with the inside of her hand.

'Everybody is well at home.'

'I don't know what to say. The devil surely has a say on earth, but he should have sympathised with you and what you did for me, Nalukwi. He should have spared me this one time. After all you did, Nalukwi, for things to end like this . . .'

'What has happened, Nasula?'

'The bag of beans, Nalukwi.'

'*Ee?*'

'Gone without one *ngwee* being paid for it. It has been stolen.'

Nalukwi fetched a slab and sat down on it, opposite Nasula. In a silence stamped with grief, Nalukwi wept. Shaking her head in disbelief, she rubbed her tears, clapped her hands and then in a low, shocked voice blunt with melancholy, she spoke. 'What bad luck is this, god of mercy?' she said. 'Are we not going to be allowed to make any progress, even with the little in our hands, from our own sweat? When we can't borrow or beg, like they who are rich? Nasula?'

She clapped her hands, made rinsing movements, and again, she wept, rubbing her tears away with the back of her right hand.

'Did it happen at night?'

'It was during the day.'

'Where you had slept?'

'There, where that stone is. That is where I had displayed the bag. It's not a long time ago that the bag was taken. I had displayed the bag. There was interest.'

Nalukwi asked the younger woman what had happened and she told her the story, describing the man who had stolen the bag of beans and his car in great detail.

'Did you see the money, note by note, when he was counting it?'

'I didn't.'

'It wasn't a bundle of real money. It must have been a bundle of paper cut from a newspaper and placed between two real notes. You should have asked him to pay you before the bag was lifted into his car.'

'It was the way he looked, Nalukwi!'

'I know. Am I not talking to say something for something to

say, like one who is mad? Do I have what to say, Nasula of ours? People know about individuals like that, and that they are many of them these days, but they still get cheated – every day and everywhere. Have you not just forgotten, maybe, that I talked about it in Swelini? Don't you remember me saying something about men who look decent and well-to-do but are something else, judging from what they do to survive?'

Nasula remembered Nalukwi's words in Swelini. The words about men of the city in suits and ties who looked like ministers or even the president himself turning into cheats and thieves. She remembered very well. The memory of the words tasted bitter.

'I have remembered. I feel bad for you, Nalukwi. How you helped me to Lusaka with that bag of beans, only for me to give it away to a thief in a suit and a tie.'

'Say it not.'

'Hmm!'

'And everyone of us so poor, no one will help with even a coin for your travel back to your home,' Nalukwi lamented. 'Just this time I have returned from the village, I found the people home with nothing to eat. Nothing. What I came with from Wimbe and Swelini is what has saved us. What are we going to do, Nasula, poor people that we are? Where are we going to find the money for your fare?'

Nasula, unable to restrain herself any more, started crying. She cried silently. Large, warm tears trickled down her cheeks, slowly, like rivers crossing a plain in search of the sea.

'Let us not go on crying,' Nalukwi consoled her and stood up. 'Nothing will come of tears. What has happened has already happened. Rise up and we will go home.'

Nasula stopped crying and stood up, wiping away the tears from her face with one end of the *citenge* she wore around her waist.

Nalukwi had brought her black travelling bag, to carry back the blanket and sheet. Nasula put the blanket, the sheet and her sackcloth bag into the hold-all and slung it over her right shoulder. Nalukwi suggested that before they go, they should try to find out if anyone at the market knew something about the man who had stolen the beans, his name or the registration number of his car.

Nasula felt lightened by the suggestion as well as being in the older friend's company. Nalukwi's head was always teeming with ideas. They bolstered your sanity and gave your mind something to cling on to at such a hopeless time as this one.

'Let us first go and talk to the man from Solwezi,' Nalukwi said and led the way, her step robust and sure as always, as though nothing in the world was the matter.

They found the man counting money, standing in front of his last three bags of beans that were leant against each other in a circle. He had sold one bag a while back, it seemed, and was trying to make sure his first counting in front of the customer had not been faulty. Recognising Nalukwi, the man made a friendly welcoming gesture, indicating that they should keep quiet until he had finished. His addition complete, he stuffed the money into the inside pocket of the jacket of the same worn, old-fashioned suit that he had been wearing the day before. He and Nalukwi shook hands over his bags of beans and exchanged enquiries about health and work. To Nasula, the man simply nodded and stood back in silence.

'What a bad thing it is that has happened,' the man broke the silence, addressing Nalukwi and staring sadly at Nasula. 'Where were you yourself?'

'At home.'

'You live in Lusaka?'

'I live in Lusaka, my home is in Mandevu. She lives in the village. We are from the same area, Mbala. We came together from the village yesterday. I had been there two weeks ago after the death of my uncle. She decided to come with me to sell that bag of beans to raise money for her school-going daughter. It was the only bag of produce that she had in the world and the only way of sending her only child to secondary school. I said, "Let us go. You will save the future of the child, even if you remain starving after you have sold the beans and sent the child to school." That is how we struggled with the bag and came here to the market.'

'Then a thing as dark as this should happen to her?'

'We are at a loss what to say. She is a widow. Here where she is, she has not a single relative in the world to look to. Her daughter of fourteen years is everything to her. She is poverty itself with no one to turn to and nowhere to clap a hand. This world is a big debt. Here we are, we cannot even find money for her to go back to the village.'

The man shook his head in pity, saying nothing, and Nalukwi changed the subject to the purpose of their visit.

'Why we have come to see you is this: I thought you might help us with some information,' she said.

'Where I can, I will.'

'The name of the man who took the bag of beans. You might have overheard someone mention it. We want to use the name to go round the market and ask about him in case someone knows him and where to find him.'

'Don't trouble yourselves.'

'The man is a hyena. He feasts on others' bones, and we must try to stop him. There is nothing wrong in trying.'

'Do you imagine that I didn't think what you are thinking, and tried to do what you are trying to do?' the man said. 'I myself have gone round the market and to the taxi rank to ask about the man. Nobody here knows him, or will say that they know him. But a customer who bought from me, and who already knew Nasula's story, had seen the man before, and he told me his name. He knew only the name. Nothing else.'

Nasula stirred, curious and excited.

'You mean you have the name of the man?' she asked.

'But the man who gave me his name, doesn't know much about him either: where he stays or what he does. He could only tell me his name. I don't know where he got it from.'

The man searched in his trouser pockets and brought out a dirty scrap of paper. He unfolded it.

'I had thought of telling you the name later, after you had settled down and rested from the bother of the crowd that had gathered round you. The name is,' he said and then reading from the paper, 'Gode Silavwe'.

He said the name a second time, more clearly, more loudly and more surely. There was something in his manner that suggested he knew from the name, that the man who had stolen the bag of beans was from the same district as the two women. He was their tribesman. Nalukwi laughed – a small sad laugh of surprise.

'Silavwe?' she repeated the thief's name and clapped her hands. 'Do you hear that name, Nasula?'

'Do I have anything to say?' Nasula replied. She thought of the man who had stolen her beans with his accursed smartness and charm.

'Is that not a name from Mbala?'

'Why do I say anything? What to say has deserted me.'

There was a moment's pause, as they all fell silent. Then the man carefully folded the piece of paper on which the thief's name was written. He gave it to Nalukwi. He had no need of it now. He had only kept the paper to make sure he gave them the correct name. Nalukwi put the piece of paper in the side pocket of the travelling bag Nasula was carrying. The young woman closed the zip of the pocket. Nalukwi turned to the man and thanked him for the information and the piece of paper.

'If it will help you, but I doubt it,' the man said. 'When I heard the name, I also knew that he was from your area because you told me, yesterday, that you were from Mbala. What I had hoped was that when you heard the name, you would either know the owner or the family from which he comes.'

Nalukwi shook her head and said she had not the smallest idea who the man could be or which family he might be from.

'We are too lowly to know people like that or what families they come from,' she added. 'We are the doormat of the world. We can be stepped on without knowing who is doing the stepping.'

'Especially true of the people of the city,' the man said, his face soft with sympathy and understanding. 'Money has roasted them into living corpses. They are not even people of their own people. A lion in the wilds is a better companion.'

'Father, we have wasted your time and blocked your beans from passers-by. We must leave you to work. You have been very kind. Let us see what more we can find out around the market. When we are tired, we will come and say goodbye before returning home.'

'I wish you good luck, friends.'

The journey turned out to be futile as the man from Solwezi had predicted it would be. No one at the market seemed to know anything about the man who had stolen the bag of beans. At midday, they gave up and returned to the man from Solwezi to say goodbye, as they had promised to do.

They found him packing his belongings. He had just sold the last of his beans and was preparing to go to the inter-city bus terminus to journey back to Solwezi that very afternoon, after he had bought himself a few things. There was an air of determination and triumph about him. Hearing his voice and words, Nasula felt happy for him and sorry for herself.

'Have you moved well?' the man asked from where he was kneeling and stuffing empty grain bags into another empty grain bag.

'Nobody has told us anything about the man,' replied Nalukwi. 'We have talked to the whole world at the market.'

'If you took so long?'

'We are on our way to my home now. We have just come to bid you farewell, as we promised.'

'You have done well to come, friends.'

The man stopped what he was doing and stood up. Carrying his stooping figure with the dignity of a popular tribal chief, he began to walk towards his clumsily pitched tent, and beckoned at Nalukwi and Nasula to follow him. He crouched under the shelter quietly and sat down on a stone facing the entrance. When Nalukwi and Nasula entered after him, he showed them an empty grain bag on which they could sit.

'Friends, it is my prayer that you will not be offended,' he said after the two women had sat down. 'Friends, we are strangers to each other, but we are children of the same creator and victims of the same fate here on earth; therefore, we are not strangers in the real sense. We are one and the same. A person who does not see the world in that way is not a human being. You and me are of one family. It is so. What happened today, your spirits and mine, have brought us together and made us one. We have come to know each other and therefore must suffer tribulation together as one family.'

His dark eyes shone with benevolence in his dusty face.

'Things like those that happened today are not things that should happen to poor people like ourselves,' he continued soberly. 'But the world is like that. So, they happen and it

93

happened. What is important is that we must not lose heart and we must help each other as members of one family.

'I am a poor man myself. I need every coin I come across. But when I heard you say that you do not even have money for the journey back to the village, I thought of keeping all the little money I have raised from the beans I came with, and my heart became heavy. I understood what the spirits were saying to me. And so, while you were going round the market, I asked some people how much is needed for one to travel to Mbala. They told me it is anything from fifteen to somewhere nearing twenty thousand *kwacha*. So I decided to give you this, mother of our children.'

He produced two ten thousand *kwacha* notes and gave them to Nasula.

A deep emotional silence reigned for a long time.

'It is a big thing you have done, father. No words will be enough,' Nalukwi said at last, and turning to Nasula: 'You can leave early in the morning tomorrow.'

Nasula nodded and she and Nalukwi on one hand, and the man on the other, began to bid each other goodbye.

Part Three

*I know no other stand than to bury
my heart in this heat without fire*

Chapter Seven

A power from the heat of loss

The bus was as black as a funeral bus. There were buses upon buses at the Lusaka inter-city terminus, but all of them and everything else, seemed invisible in the black of that bus. It was as though the tongues of its black would swallow you and turn you into darkness. That was how black that bus was. Like death.

The woman sat on the concrete floor of the station, hunched round her knees, against one of the pillars that supported the roof of the large station building. She was waiting to get into the black bus to make her journey home to face the death of hope: the horror that would turn her offspring from being a vibrant scholar into an ordinary poverty-stricken village girl without a future. She sat alone apart from everybody, wrung and bitter with anger and despair.

Hate and fear sat behind her dark eyes like witches. Dangerous thoughts in the caverns of her being beat down upon her parched soul. She wanted to die. She had to go back to the village but she did not want to go. She had accepted that she must go. But now at this last hour, she did not want to leave the place which owned the death of her daughter's future. She felt she would prefer to die than go home and be confronted by the sight of Sula. Why couldn't the ground beneath her collapse, thus saving her the pain of a long journey made monstrous with disappointment?

Cold derisive laughter broke out in the blackness of he soul. Nasula, what is this, woman? What is becoming of you? Wishing for your own death? Stop being foolish. Place yourself under the shadow of your gods and spirit. Do you think there is a woman anywhere who is wholly happy? If there is, that woman must be stupid. Nasula, only imbeciles and sweet idiots have a life whose happiness does not hang in the balance. A true woman with such a life does not exist. Stop being foolish. Just look your troubles in the eye and stop longing for your own death. Nasula, don't be childish. The world has not ended.

Something stung her eyes. Bitter, unashamed tears. Not cried out, but held back – hot, molten. No. She would not let herself die. She did not want to die. The child. What about the child? Sula, her only one? What would become of her without a mother, without anyone in the whole world?

The dust of her torment rose into a whirlwind, absorbing her in a violent rotation. The earth crumbled, hurling her birdlike into darkness to the land of the dead where death was not. At last there was stillness and peace and silence.

A weight dropped on to her body. A germination and a growing in her womb, then a violent pain. The pain, red and hot, tore into her. She dissolved into nothingness and there was a birth. She came to and found Sula, no longer a baby but a young woman. The woman embraced her daughter, shedding tears of love and joy. Then the cloud of illusion lifted. She felt devastation.

The woman came out of her daydreaming and found it was not the body of her daughter that she was in contact with but the cold concrete of one of the pillars supporting the roof of the bus shelter. She was in tears but these were not the streams of tears that fell in her dream. They were drops at the doors of her eyes. They were not tears of love and joy, but tears of sorrow and hate.

'Mother of Sula.' It was the boy Nalukwi had given her to see her safely off. Ntazana, as the boy was called, was standing in front of her. She saw the boy from his tattered blue canvas shoes to the thighs of his oversized, dirty blue jeans. She fought her tears back, blinked heavily, then looked up, easing her hunched shoulders.

'The ticket and the change,' the boy said, stretching the hand in which he was holding the ticket and the change out to her.

'You have bought the ticket? As far as Senga?'

'They have written it on the ticket. Lusaka to Senga Hill.'

She took the ticket and the change from the boy and knotted them in a corner of the *citenge* she was wearing. It was the one that Nalukwi had first lent and then given her. She tucked the knot away at her waist.

'Thank you for the work you have done,' she said when she was through. 'Go home now.'

'Mother said I should not leave the station before the bus you board leaves.'

'Let me not hold you; everything will be well.'

'The bus is half full. Look there. It will not be long before you leave. It's not a long time that I'll have to wait.'

'Don't worry, child. Go home and play. I shall have no problems. Greet your mother and everybody at home for me. Go well, child.'

The boy left. The black of the bus flooded her eyes. Loneliness and aloneness multiplied the stir and bustle of the station into a deafening roar. She did not dissolve back into the peace of her imagined world, where existence turned into non-existence and suffering disappeared. She clung on to the sooty foil of the outside world, watching what was happening around her with the plaintive eye of a guinea fowl.

The whitish molten gold of the sun was so high in the limpid sky, it had to be noon. It was fiercely bright and hot outside the bus shelter.

She had been at the station for a long time waiting for the bus to fill with passengers before it could set off. That was what happened in these days of the nineties. In the past, people slept at bus stations because there were not enough buses. Now people still slept at stations. Not because there were no buses, but because there were more than enough, and a bus would only leave the station when it was full, and now, in the nineties, there were not so many passengers to fill a bus quickly.

A loud, shrill voice tore the air like the jagged edge of a saw. It was the voice of a scrawny young man without a garment on the upper half of his body.

'Mpulungu via Mbala ... Mpulungu via Mbala ...' the young man was yelling, referring to the destination of the black bus. The cause of this burst of shouting was a group of new arrivals, which he had just spotted at a distance: men and women laden with bags, suitcases and bundles of possessions wrapped in cloth. The group was far away, but one could see that they had their eyes on the black bus.

It was the only one loading for Mpulungu. Yet, hearing the young itinerant shouting its destination, you would have thought a thousand other buses were competing with it. And seeing the way he gesticulated, and paced about, how he signalled to the bus and made sure you knew where it was; you would have thought the bus was not a conspicuous monster, not one so black that it blunted your retina, but a colourless miniature vehicle hidden by the multitude of other buses.

'Mpulungu ... Mbala ... Mpulungu ...' the dirty, scrawny, human cicada cried on in the thick station wilderness, swinging round, thumping his feet and pointing at the black bus; sweating, panting like a hungry dog, spit forming at the corners of his wide mouth as if he suffered from epilepsy.

'Mpulungu via Mbala, Mpulungu ... Mbala ... Mpulungu – Mpulungu – Mpulungu!'

His friends, other equally dishevelled young men, saw what he had seen. They sallied forth and joined in. Their messages and signals were different, unique to each of them, but still in consonance with each other, a pure amplified chorus of shouting, yelling and gesticulation.

Abaleya, abaleya, abaleya . . .

Abali busy, *abali* busy, *abali* busy . . .

Washala, abaleya!

The young men were personified madness. A few did sound and look lethargic, but the power in the throats and movements of the rest was that of a demon. Nasula wondered at the power of their lungs. But she did not lack understanding of the young men's world. She understood. None of those criers was a driver or conductor. They were shouting and scurrying about to win the hearts of the driver and the conductor of each bus. So that when it was full and time for departure, they would be given 'something with which to buy a drink and what to eat'.

She was also aware that some did what they did to create confusion among the travellers, so they could steal from them unnoticed, undetected.

She was a woman of the village but she knew these things. She understood many of the ways of the towns. The young men did these things, young women did worse. No, young women did not do worse. They allowed worse things to be done to them for money, or in order to make it possible for them to steal money from drunken men. Nameless things worse than *punku*. They showed their flesh around and let men do the most terrible things to them. Bad things worthy of a dog. Without an education, she would not allow Sula, her daughter, to come to the towns.

Sula to come here, to the city, and become the rubbish pit for every rotten stick in the woods? If Sula disobeyed her and fled away from the village to the town, she would kill herself the day she knew it. *Eh*, Nasula, to lose your only one like that?

The group that the scrawny young man had spotted drew near the black bus and into the jaws of the criers. They shared them out like precious pieces of food, offering to chaperone them to the place where the tickets were sold by the door of the bus and to help them with what they were carrying. Some of the travellers yielded to willing hands, others cringed suspiciously and refused to be chaperoned or helped with their luggage. But there was maddening commotion around all of them.

They were about six in number, rugged men and women of the countryside. As the last one of the group joined the small queue of those who were buying tickets, the commotion died down, and the criers withdrew, like hounds after a furious fit of barking at a welcome visitor to the master's home.

Time passed. The criers screamed that only two more passengers were needed before the bus was full and ready to leave. Nasula shook away her thoughts and looked up in the direction of the black bus. The people that had been buying tickets had disappeared, the ticketed passengers, who had been sauntering around the station, returned and were getting into the bus. The loaders were rolling a yellow tent over the mountain of luggage on the roof carrier.

'Two – Mpulungu – *abaleya* . . .'

'*Abali* busy, two Mpulungu *apo*!'

Her thoughts stirred. It was true, the bus was almost full. The time to go had come. She would go. What could she do? She had to go, although she did not feel like going away from the place where her loss had occurred. Thinking of the loss and her impending journey, she suddenly felt as if her sojourn at the station, sitting against the concrete pillar, had been a rest before the storm. Her last act on earth before meeting her creator. Her last breath before being confronted with death.

She grew into a rock too heavy for the winds of panic to move. The concrete beneath her became a swamp, her feet sank into its cold, sticky mud. How would she rise and trudge through the mud to the mouth of the bus?

Now the criers announced that the bus was full and everybody with a ticket should board. The bus roared into life, trembling, and churning out grey clouds of smoke. A sharp coldness speared her heart and weighed it down bleeding. Her heart contracted and began to throb with the tension of fear and grief: a stillness, silence and darkness fell upon her.

'I saw someone giving you a ticket.' It was the scrawny crier without a shirt on his back who was talking to her, standing in front of her, with a quizzical look in his small, beady eyes. 'You are travelling, are you not?'

'I am travelling,' she heard herself say in a voice that crepitated as if it had fallen into disuse.

'But not on this bus, the black one?'

'That is the one I am to travel on.'

'What then are you waiting for? This bus is leaving. It is about to go. What are you waiting for?'

She did not talk or look at the young man again. Silently, calling every grain of her will power, she gathered herself to her feet and, clutching at the cord of her sackcloth bag which was slung over her shoulder, she climbed into the black bus. Her eyes were fogged as she found her way along the passage between the columns of grey steel seats and through the other passengers still standing in the aisle. Everything was visible to her only as vague shadows or silhouettes. But she could feel the thrust of their looks like spears piercing her body.

A chasm appeared on her left, between two sets of seats, a couple of rows before the back seat. All the three seats there were not occupied. She slumped into the seat next to the window. A blackness swamped her immediately. She was not

103

there when the bus started to move. Trees, grass and hills, not the glass and concrete jungle of the city, were disappearing in the opposite direction when she looked through the window on her right.

That was the reality before her. The blue sky, the green bush. She, Nasula the suffering woman, was on a black bus travelling to the village where her daughter waited for her with impatient eyes. She was on her way back to Swelini.

The woman glared at the journey ahead of her. It was a long journey with many towns to pass through: Kabwe, Kapiri-Mposhi, Mkushi, Serenje, Mpika and Kasama. After Kasama, a stone's throw before Mbala, she would alight at Senga Hill, which was not a town but just a post, and walk in the direction of the rising sun, to Swelini, her home village. It was a long journey but a short one for her. To her, the journey was just a few steps' worth of travel.

The journey would last the rest of that day, the whole of the night and part of the following day. It would be nearing noon the next day before she set foot at Senga Hill. It was a long journey but to her, it would be gone in the flash of a witch's journey on a broom across the sky. So short a journey that she could already smell and feel the squalor and loneliness of her yard, her hut. She could already see the plaintive sight of her daughter.

But the bus was oblivious of her world and the torment in her heart. Decrepit though it was, it sang and danced along in celebration of the catch it had made – the conductor had been heard boasting that the bus was mostly full of people going to Mpulungu, and not of people dropping off on the way. Aaah! the money it had hauled for its masters. The monster was in a happy mood. It ate the distance before it with the frank alacrity of young wolves.

She hated the bus. How could she not hate it? The monster,

in all its posture and boisterousness, so eagerly taking her back to her daughter. Little did it know or care that it was taking her to a graveyard.

Of course nothing in her life was the fault of the bus. Nevertheless, she still had a cause to hate it because it was taking her back home. She also hated it because it seemed afflicted with an insatiable joy that she was among those who had boarded it and given it a reason to set off. That she had paid for the ride on it, so that its owner could have money to pay for the schooling of his or her children while her own daughter stayed at home, in the village, because she, her mother, had no money to send her to school.

Still, the bus was happy and indifferent and it sped on, singing, dancing, laughing, faster than a duiker would, and as though it were not an old, ragged monster.

The road was good. It was wide and smooth. It was a new road, a road of the nineties. It was a glittering, tarred road with neat, shiny white lines marking its demarcations. The black bus was evidently enjoying moving along that road. It was a very good road indeed.

'These are the roads to travel on. You should have seen what it was like in the old days,' a man's voice could be heard somewhere behind her; another replied, 'If all roads were like this, Zambia would be heaven on earth.'

'It's a dangerous road,' said another.

'How do you mean?'

'It's too smooth, a good road has a rough surface that holds the tyres of the vehicles. This one is as slippery as a snake's belly.'

'Are you a road builder?'

'Have you not heard the many stories about vehicles that have rolled over on this road? Ask anyone who has used it many times. They will tell you stories that will make you ill.'

'Are you missing the potholes and sharp bends of its past then?'

'The old road was something else; but this one is no good either. It is good that the new government is working hard to better our roads, but it should be careful not to let the contractors it hires make more roads like this one.'

'Nothing is good in the world.'

'Some things are good, but not this road,' said the second man with a closing edge to his voice. 'This road is deadly. Many vehicles have skidded to their ruin because of the surface on this road, especially during the rainy season. Let it rain and see what will happen to you, if you don't drive at the pace of a snail. This road is a snake in the grass.'

The conversation ended there. Nasula laughed deep in her heart. Who would see with naked eyes that such a good road was so full of danger? Everything in the world was good and bad at the same time. In some of them goodness was more than badness and in others, badness outweighed goodness. That was the only difference. The problem was how to tell what was what.

She remembered the man who had stolen her bag of beans. So good-looking, so apparently honest. Who would see the snake in such an open face, such friendliness? People who look good can still bring misery to someone. They can kill you. Had the man who had stolen her beans not as good as killed her?

The road inclined steeply upwards. The bus sneezed, coughed and began to sing with a new power. It clattered, whined and ululated: loudly, mournfully, tunefully. Nasula clenched her teeth. Her heart was throbbing, her head reeling with sorrow. She sorrowed until her head ached. The aching in the head grew into a vortex. In it, a stone would have been crushed to powder. But the bus saw nothing of this. It moved and sang with more and more emotion.

106

All the other passengers were eating, chatting, jesting, men and women alike; boys, girls and children. They ate, joked and laughed. Everyone present was alive with an occupation. They passed each other things, handing over the larger items such as a basket or a bag, and just throwing the smaller ones such as a box of matches. They exchanged food and helped each other with change. They did everything under the sun. It was like a market place. Nasula alone was still and silent, buried in the sorrows of her loss. Mute and stiff as a corpse.

The thought of the man who had stolen her bag of beans, the thought of her loss and what it meant to her, and the thought of that empty, promiseless journey home. These burned every tissue and nerve into ashy striations.

The distance left behind had grown. They were over half way to the first town, Kabwe. A whirlwind was born inside her, filling her with an unearthly power – a confusion of hate, love and passion. Her being spun and floated in anguish, fear and rage. Images germinated and blossomed, clear images, precise, detailed. She began to see with a sense beyond seeing, to hear with a sense beyond hearing, and to feel with a sense beyond feeling. Her mind expanded to unrealisable limits. She acquired extra senses and abilities: determination, resoluteness and clarity.

The world became cold. Too cold. Her world. She started shivering. She trembled like a reed in a fast-flowing river. She was alone in the middle of a plain, a vast expanse of emptiness. She dissolved out of herself and stood apart, watching herself and the cold, darkish sands of the plain. She saw herself at its centre, alone, seated on a stool of life and death, her feet partially buried in the sand.

A hearth appeared before her from nowhere. She stretched her arms over it to warm herself. There was a heat coming from it. But when she tried to stir the fire into more life, she discovered there was no fire. Not a twig of firewood. Horror-stricken, she drew herself closer to the hearth and in a loud, silent, suffering voice she cried out: spirits of the dead, help me, I know of no other way than to bury my heart in this heat without fire.

Suddenly, her head collided with something hard and cold. She came out of her illusion. She had hit her head hard on the steel at the back of the seat in front of her. The bus had suddenly jerked to a halt and made her fall heavily forward.

'Road-block . . . road-block . . .' voices in the bus were saying, pronouncing the reason why the bus had stopped. 'It's a road-block.'

She looked up, and through the fog of her eyes, she saw several policemen and a blue light flashing authoritatively in front of the bus, to the right.

'Road-block, road-block,' she whispered to herself, her head and heart swelling with anxiety. 'This is the chance.'

She had made up her mind without knowing it. Now she just acted. Rigidly obeying her impulse, enthusiastically, without equivocation. She jerked to her feet and mumbled an excuse to the other passengers on the same seat. The passengers, both women she had not bothered to look at, to know what kind of people they were. Before the women could answer and give her way, she had squeezed passed into the main aisle and was hurrying towards the front of the bus with so much force and disregard for the world around her that everybody noticed and watched in amazement.

'What's wrong with her?'

'Does she want to vomit?'

'Look there, people, what is it with that woman?'

And so on and so forth. But nothing touched her hard enough to jolt her into feeling ashamed or shy. It was all too faint and confused. The noise that the other passengers in the bus raised, did not mean anything to her. She knew and thought only of her decision. As she drew abreast of the passenger's door on her left, she called the conductor and halted abruptly at the edge of the stairway below, looking around. Every eye in the bus was drawn to her, but this reality meant nothing to Nasula.

'Where is the conductor?' she asked, her eyes searching round with anxiety. 'Where is he sitting?'

'He is outside the bus,' a voice said somewhere nearby. 'Didn't you see him getting out just now?'

She turned towards the door and only then noticed that the door was ajar and some of the people on the bus had alighted.

'Conductor,' she called as she stepped out of the bus. 'Where are you? Conductor?'

A tall young man in a black jeans suit materialised and loomed before her, a few steps in front of the door of the bus, his face a billowing brown moon with huge brown eyes.

'What can I help you with, I am the conductor.'

'Give me back my money, I want to remain here.' She untied the knot at the end of the *citenge* she was wearing, pulled out the ticket and held it out to the conductor, after she had tied the knot and tucked it back at her waist. 'Here is the ticket. Take out your share of the money and give me the rest.'

'No, why? I can't waste a seat for such a long distance.'

'I have troubles I cannot explain to you. It is not madness that is making me say what I am saying. Understand and let me remain here.'

'You are free to remain, but I won't give you the money and waste a seat for so many miles.'

'It is not my wish to trouble you or want you to waste a seat,' she insisted, beseechingly. 'If I had a way I would forget about the money, but I am a woman of no means and a big problem has afflicted me. I have no other money to use apart from what I paid you for this ticket.'

'Petrol is expensive these days. You shouldn't have come on the bus if you knew you had a problem.'

'I plead with you.'

The conductor shook his head decidedly and began to walk away. The engine of the bus started running and she heard the sneezing sound of the gear being engaged. A darkness fell upon her. She dropped to her knees in a prayerful posture and started sobbing, clutching her bag of sackcloth to her chest emotionally as if it was a baby that had just died.

The bus driver saw this. He asked the conductor what the matter was and the conductor explained.

'Where is her ticket to?'

'Mbala, at Senga Hill.'

'This man here is going to Kapiri-Mposhi,' the driver said, referring to an elderly man standing below him at the door to the cabin of the bus. Let him take her seat, we should be able to find someone going to Mbala or Kasama at Kapiri. Give her back the money.'

The conductor, irked and reluctant, stepped down from the bus and walked towards the woman. He brought out a thick, folded bundle of notes from the side pocket of his trousers. Unfolding the bundle, he pulled out three five thousand *kwacha* notes and held them out to the woman without saying anything. The blurred sight of the money in the conductor's extended hand relieved her heart of some of its pain. The woman stopped sobbing and took the notes from the conductor.

She put the money away in her *citenge*. The policemen at the road-block, the passengers in the black bus, and onlookers watched, mesmerised by the sight of Nasula. After she had put away the money, she remained kneeling and began to wipe her face with the end of the *citenge*.

The man who was to take her seat came running towards the bus from where he had gone to collect his luggage. The conductor was waiting impatiently for him by the door. The man arrived panting and bent under the weight of the bag he was carrying in his hand. He and the conductor entered the bus and the conductor closed the door after them. The bus roared, trembled, and left.

On the other side of the road, a small, new white minibus, which had just passed the road-block, stopped, and a voice in it cried out 'Lusaka'. Nasula sprang up. Slapping the dust from her knees, she traversed the road and climbed into the immaculate, petite little beast. She was its only catch. The minibus jerked into motion as soon as she was on its stairway. The only free seat was right by the door. She sat down and settled into her journey back to Lusaka. The fog and chaff in her head had cleared. She saw clearly why she was going back to the city.

Chapter Eight

The bone and flesh of evil is a strong limb

At the hearth of her ambitions and desires, a fire of hope had burned from one solitary twig; this lay in the reality of her one bag of beans. Evil had struck, the devil knew from where. The beautiful man had come and tricked her out of the bag. Now there wasn't a single twig in the hearth. The fire had turned to ashes. To nothing. The hearth was empty.

Yet a little warmth remained in the smoke-darkened cooking stones. She drew closer to the hearth, warming herself. She became a rock. She was determined, inhaling the invisible dust of its poison, determined to fight for the welfare of her only child; to hunt for the man who had stolen her bag of beans. This was the reason why she was returning to Lusaka.

The minibus wound its way through the Lusaka inter-city bus terminus and reached its final destination. She alighted and headed straight for Kamwala market not a long distance away. She did not know why she had decided to begin her search from the spot where the theft had taken place. She didn't believe the market vendors would provide her with useful information, or that the man who had stolen her beans would be so foolish as to return so soon after his act of trickery.

She did not even really know what she was doing, or how to search for the man who had stolen her bag of beans. She only desired to hunt him down. Even if she did so blindly and without hope.

At Kamwala market, she began at the area where produce was sold in bulk. She searched, inquired, and took inspection of anyone who looked anything like the man she was looking for;

she peered at every yellow car she saw and at whoever was in it. She scoured the place almost mindless of where she was, what she was doing, and what onlookers might think of her. She was alone in the world. When she had exhausted that section, she proceeded to search through other areas of the market.

She was just leaving the sector in which vegetables were sold, and walking towards the furniture section, when someone called after her. She stopped and turned to face an old man who was short, thin and ragged, with tufted grey hair and a disfigured face. 'Are you not the woman who was cheated of her bag of beans yesterday, the woman who came from Mbala?' the old man said when he was standing in front of her.

'I am the one,' she answered, anxious.

'I have remembered you. Yes, it is you,' continued the old man. 'What a sad thing it is that happened to you. God will punish that man. What I am saying is true. A day will come when each of us will be punished for the wrongs that we have done in our lives. That man will cry like a train one day. It's me who is telling you, God will treat him for what he is – a shameless thief.'

'What do you know about the man?'

'His name is Gode. His family name has gone, but it is one of these names from your area, the ones every Mambwe-speaking person has, the ones that start with si. He is very much from your area. He is a man from Mbala. Your tribesman. Come to think of it, how could your own tribesman do something like that to someone like you, here, in the capital city, so far away from your homeland? His family name has just gone but it is a Mambwe name. He is: Si . . . Si . . .'

'Silavwe.'

'That is the name, so you even know his name?'

'I have been told his name by others. What I want to know now is where he stays.'

'Ah, sister of mine,' the old man said and chuckled, sounding amused. 'Do you think a man like that would tell anyone where he stays? They don't even tell the ones they sleep with, in the hotel rooms they buy with stolen money. Do people like that ever stay in one place? Are they not like moles that don't live in the same tunnel all their lives?

'People like that have too many things to run away from. They won't tell anybody where they stay. The only ones who might know where they stay most of the time are their very close friends, who also cheat people out of things. Do you expect such friends to tell you anything?

'I thought you had gone back to the village. Why haven't you gone 'til now?'

'I have something to do before I can go.'

'Good woman, I can see you are very troubled. But hear me well. If the man who took your beans is the reason for your not returning where you have come from, don't waste your time. You will never find him, and if you find him, you will never catch him, and if you catch him, you will never get the better of him.'

'Thank you. I have heard what you have said,' she said quietly, no longer interested in the conversation, and wanting to be left alone.

'If you think that I am cheating you or don't know what I am talking about, go and look for him.'

'I have heard you.'

'A man who does what that man did to an innocent woman like you is not a person to go hunting for. He will just take out a gun and shoot you, or run over you with his car.'

A cold wave swept through Nasula as she imagined facing the man who had stolen her beans, as he, in a furious mood, wanted to kill her. She knew there was nothing she could do in her own defence. But she had a journey to travel and the passion within

114

her drove her onward, and urged her to find the man who had stolen her bag of beans. And she listened and surrendered herself to this feeling and reassured herself that she would hunt for the man to the end of the world.

'Thank you for your words, good-day.'

'Take my advice, go back to the village quickly. I know what I am talking about. Lusaka is a place of madness and Gode is a terror. I wish you well, good-day.'

'Thank you.'

What did it matter if Gode was death itself. The man had stolen her only hope of salvation, which lay in her daughter's schooling. She must look for him and she would pursue him to her death, if that was what he wanted. The pain of her loss called to her and she would rise to its call.

From the area of furniture, she went into the main market building where dried fish and *kapenta* were sold. After that she went to the section for *salaula* and next, to the section for new clothes. So she went on from one area to another, until there was nowhere in the market to which she had not been. She found herself standing before the taxi rank, facing the long line of shops across the road to the east, staring at every yellow car that pulled up or passed by with a keen eye.

The complete unexpectedness of events dazed her. But she was not dreaming. Someone had mentioned the name Gode, someone near the place where she was standing. She looked round with attentive ears and guessed that what she had heard, must have come from one of the three young men standing beside a red taxi. She went and stood near the group without being noticed. They were smart, good-looking young men with naughty faces and on the talkative side. She could not tell what it was that they were saying exactly, but there was something of Gode's shadow about the young men.

'I know where he lives,' one of them said. He was the tallest of the three and was standing between his two friends, leaning against the front door of the red car, his arms folded over his chest. 'I have gone to his home many times. Gode and I are very close if you don't know.'

'Sure?' the one wearing a hat, replied, his voice and countenance full of admiration.

'Gode and I have done deals together if you want to know. Big, hot deals for that matter.'

'It's only now that I am knowing that you are that close to Gode.'

'Where do you think I got the money I used to buy this car? It's from a deal Gode and I did together.'

Nasula swallowed. She could not hold herself silent any more. She walked to the group and greeted them.

'The name Gode interests me in what I overheard you saying,' she said when the three young men had answered her greeting and were staring at her with questioning eyes. 'Could it be Gode Silavwe that you are talking about?'

'He is the one we are talking about. Is he your relative?' the one with a black hat answered her.

'I am his aunt from the village . . .'

At that moment, the young man to the left of the one with a black hat pulled the latter aside behind the car. After a tête-à-tête, the two returned, looking suddenly indifferent, and in a hurry to leave.

'You say you are related to Gode Silavwe?' the one with a hat said to her and speared her with a sidelong glance, his long dark face somewhat averted.

'I said I am his aunt from the village,' she agreed, no longer sure of herself and suspicious.

'Woman! Don't lie, you are not talking to children,' the one who had pulled aside the one with the hat, interjected with sudden heat. He took a step closer towards her and stared at her with scolding dark eyes. 'Why do you lie? Are you not the woman who lost a bag of beans yesterday? Here, at this market? You think I don't know you?'

'It's true what you have said,' Nasula said shyly, feeling ashamed of having been caught telling a lie. She was not used to telling lies. 'I am the woman whose bag of beans was stolen at this market yesterday. I want you to help me.'

'Help you with what?'

'I want you to tell me and show me where Gode Silavwe stays.'

'Did I tell you that I know where a man by the name of Gode Silavwe stays? Did I tell you I know anyone by that name?'

'Your friend here, he knows,' Nasula said, pointing at the one with a brown jeans suit and a hat.

'Who told you I know the man you are talking about?' the one with a hat said, grinning defensively.

'But you said it yourself, here, that you have been to Gode's home many times.'

'Which Gode?'

'The Gode that we are talking about. Silavwe. Gode Silavwe.'

'Woman, spare me the breath. The person you are talking about is not the person I was talking about. Is the Gode you are talking about the only Gode and Silavwe in the world?'

'Then tell me and show me where the Gode that you were talking about stays.'

'Of what business is he to you?'

'He ran away with my bag of beans.'

'Where were you for someone to run away with your bag of beans, a whole bag? Woman, leave us to talk about other things. Go and attend to more important matters. I don't know anyone by the name of Gode and I am not a one to know where every other person in this town stays. Go away from here.'

Nasula hung her head in disbelief. Then everything happened

in a flash. When she looked up, the man in a brown jeans suit and a black hat was driving away and his two friends had disappeared into thin air. It was as if it were a dream when happenings vanish without any logical conclusion. Just as in the fable about a human being and a chameleon. The former saw the chameleon and said, 'Chameleon, I have seen you.'

'Are you sure?' chameleon asked.

'Why not?' the human being said.

Whereupon chameleon asked the human being what colour he, the chameleon, was. And before the human could open his mouth, the chameleon had changed his colours more often than the human could follow. And the next thing the human being knew was that there was no chameleon anywhere.

The car belonging to the young man who knew Gode Silavwe had disappeared. Nasula awoke from the dizziness of shock and disappointment and found a ragged man who looked like a tramp standing before her. He was a man in middle age, dark, stooped, with a thick moustache and small humour-infested eyes.

'He was not telling the truth,' the man said, enunciating his words carefully, and showing his greenish teeth and unhealthy, red gums. 'I listened to your conversation with them. The three of them know Gode very well and they know where to find him. The trouble is no one in this town will tell you anything about Gode, or where he stays or where you can find him. Not even a policeman. They fear Gode might find out and then Lusaka will become too small for them.'

'Do you know where he stays yourself?'

'Would I want to know?' the man said and looked round with excited eyes, almost jumping as he did so, as if Gode were a snake on which he had just stepped. 'I wouldn't want to know; it would haunt me. Good lady of the soil, I am here where I stand to plead with you to go back to where you came

118

from and not waste time looking for Gode, because nothing will come from your effort. You are even lucky it's only one bag he cheated you out of. Eh, one bag! What is one bag with Gode?'

His narrow eyes darting with laughter, he clapped his hands and shook his shrunken head in surprised amusement.

'Gode Silavwe has come to this market in the past, with a truck and a trailer and filled it to the top with beans that were not his, but belonged to strangers who were selling them at the market. He told them he was transporting the bags to a collection point because he had won a tender to supply beans. He told them that he was going to the bank to collect the money to pay for the beans they had loaded on to the truck. Did those people not wait until they gave up and returned to where they had come from? Did they find Gode? Even if they had, what would they have done to him? Nothing. That son of a miracle goes ahead and collects the money from whomever he supplied the beans to and eats it.'

She did not say anything. She just nodded at the man in frustration and crossed the road to the line of shops and continued with her search for Gode, who was now something more of an unpleasant mystery, after what she had heard about him.

The sun went down behind the horizon and dusk was gathering. Shops and offices had closed and the streets were deserted. She was in the middle of the main area of Kamwala shopping centre. Her feet were heavy, her legs shaky and her body weak from exhaustion, hunger and thirst. She was a lump of fatigue, sweating and dusty. But she clung to her last flicker of strength and started towards the inter-city bus terminus in the north.

She crossed the big road from the town centre, and walked down the road towards the bus station. The gates to the terminus finally appeared on her left. She by-passed the first gate and pushed into the station through the second one, carefully

119

picking her way through the crowd, afraid she might fall down at the slightest contact with someone.

She went to the cluster of wooden stalls where beverages were sold. There was one that was deserted but for one boy who was the vendor. It attracted her. She ordered a cup of tea and a bun. The boy did a mental calculation and told her three hundred and fifty *kwacha* was what she would have to pay. A hundred and fifty for the tea and two hundred for the bun. She nodded acknowledgement and the boy showed her a place where she could sit, a wood and animal skin stool before a shaky wooden table that looked more like a bench.

Slowly, narrowing her eyes in discomfort, she lowered herself on to the stool. The pain of fatigue surged through her body and limbs. She closed her eyes. The darkness was a relief. A while later, she heard something make a dull sound, and saw a purple plastic cup containing a dark, steaming liquid on a plastic plate of such a faded colour that it was difficult to tell whether it was yellow or brown. Next to the cup on the same plate was a bun. The boy had just put them on the table, right below her bowed head, which she held in her hands.

She tore a piece from the bun, dipped it into the tea and began to eat and drink. She finished them in no time.

'Give me some water to drink,' she said to the boy, undoing the knot at the end of her *citenge* where she kept her money.

The boy gave her some water and when she had drunk it and paid for the tea and the bun, she stood up with much effort and started looking for a place to sleep at the station.

She decided on a place next to a pillar at the south-western end of the bus shelter and away from the rest of the crowd. The place looked like one that no one had ever been interested in. It reeked with dust and litter. She fetched pieces of cardboard and swept a small clearing. After she had thrown the rubbish away, she spread her *citenge* on the floor, and using her bag of sack-cloth as a pillow, and having nothing to cover herself with, she lay down – a heap of aching joints – hearing and seeing little of the world around her.

She awoke as the sun was rising with new strength. Up on her feet, she picked up her bag and slung it over her shoulder. Then she shook out the *citenge*, wrapped it round her waist and sat down to wait for the day to grow a little more. When the sun was higher in the sky, she started off towards the town centre, without eating or drinking anything, and without washing her face or cleaning her teeth.

She was heading west along the busy tarred road from the Civic Centre. A roundabout with a water fountain at its centre appeared to her left; next she passed a tall steel and concrete building; then she turned right and proceeded northwards, towards Cairo Road, the most famous street in the land, the busiest vein through the heart of the capital city. It was a long walk through streams of people wrapped in their own small worlds.

And so for the rest of the day she walked, looked, crossed this road, turned down that, paused before a yellow car, started at the sight of someone who looked like Gode, and on and on, until the sun went down. Then again weary, thirsty and hungry, she went back to the inter-city bus terminus, bought a bun and a cup of tea as her supper and only meal, and then slept in the same place and same way as she had the previous night.

Almost a whole week passed. She continued with her search, without any sign of success. During that time, she visited many parts of town: several shanty compounds, low- and medium-density residential areas, revisiting the places she thought were more promising as she found it necessary. She had lost much weight and was very thin. She had also become very dirty, smelly, and sticky with sweat for she had not been able to wash. And she was so frail and stiff that she could not move for a long distance without sitting down to rest.

The acceptance of defeat began to creep over her. She could feel that her strength and will were waning. Again and again, a ghost in the wilderness of her being whispered admonitions to her, urging her to give up and go back to the village. She would listen and say to herself: gods, spirits of the dead, is this your will? If it is your will, yes, let me return home before I go mad or die. And she would weep emotionally.

But a power she could not overcome, which was from a bleeding heart, told her not to listen to the whispers of discouragement, or give up when she had already suffered so much. It urged her on. To this power she yielded while at the same time allowing the ghost of defeat to haunt her. She struggled on, a thin, valiant, invisible thread pulling her along in the direction of nowhere.

It was the Friday following the Friday she had arrived in Lusaka. The sun was boiling whitish, bright and hot. She was walking along Cairo Road, on the eastern side, heading south.

A large empty space on her left appeared between a building with a glass finish and a bank. The empty space lay before a large cream building, which looked like a box of matches, and had red writing on its façade. The cream building housed a shop for the small things of the home, like food and utensils. It was a new shop in the city and in the country. It came from South Africa and was named Shoprite Checkers. In Zambia it was a shop of the nineties: neat, colourful and well stocked, unlike the drab, poverty-ridden semblance of a shop for things of the home that the building had once housed.

The nineties. The years of the rule of money. The years of havelessness, bad rains and the new disease. The harsh years of madness and evil!

The empty space in front of Shoprite was where those who had come to buy from the shop left vehicles under the eyes of the shop's security guards. It was a good place for one to sit down and take a rest without being noticed as many people came and went, paused and moved on, for one reason or another all the time. She had sat and rested there three times during the past few days without any embarrassment and she wondered if she should do so again.

She entered the Shoprite yard and sat down on what had become her usual place. This was on the kerb that marked the northern boundary of the shop's yard, facing the exit into Cairo Road at the southern end of the yard. Vehicles, mainly cars, parked outside the shop, and a crowd of people moved in and out, many carrying red and yellow plastic bags; they spread before her like a sea. A multicoloured sea, sharp and shiny in the hot, bright sun.

The body ached and itched almost unbearably. She felt sweat dripping down her armpits and slithering down her rib-cage. Her breathing began to settle down and she began to doze, unable to restrain herself.

She had no idea how much time had passed. But she caught herself breathing as one about to fall asleep. Not wanting to, she stood up. Just then, she saw it and weariness left her instantly. She was suddenly wide-awake. Invigorated. At first she felt disbelief, then a deluge of reassurance that this indeed was the one – the yellow car belonging to Gode, who had stolen her bag of beans.

There was no doubt about it. She had not seen it arriving, but there it was, parked ahead of her, to the right. There was nobody inside.

She shuddered. Anxiety and bitterness threatened to overwhelm her. She dissolved into confusion at the centre of which was just the yellow car. Careful not to take her eyes off it, she lowered herself into a squatting position behind a dustbin to hide herself from her adversary.

At that moment a short man with a pot-belly, wearing a white singlet and blue trousers, strutted towards the car from the opposite direction and stood by the driver's door. Her heart sank. This man was not the thief.

But much time passed and the man did not get into the car and drive off. She decided he was not the owner of the car, or the one driving it, and that he had come just to wait for whoever. She felt a breeze of sudden relief and she waited for the lion to appear. And it happened, just like a dream.

Smartly dressed in a black suit, the familiar figure of Gode appeared with a Shoprite bag in his right hand. With a bouncy step he strutted towards the car, threw the plastic bag into the boot and planted himself before the short man with a pot-belly.

The two men shook hands and started chatting. Blood rushed to her brow, and she felt something like fire in her eyes, which blinded her momentarily. It passed like lightning. She stood up, uttering a cry. Sula her cowrie of hope. With the rapidity of lightning she undid and did her *citenge* round her waist. Her fatigue was gone. In another moment, she was standing before the two men. The idea of striking down the spiteful thief streaked through her mind, but she swallowed and regained her self-control. Then she coughed deliberately, to attract the men's attention and when Gode turned and faced her, she looked him straight in the eye.

'Have I not found you?' she said courageously. 'You thought I would not find you, but I have found you. Have I not found you?'

Gode Silavwe stared at her lengthily, thoughtfully. Afterwards, he shrugged in dissent and frowned unknowingly.

'Who are you?' he said, smoothing his spotlessly clean, pinkish white shirt over his belly. 'Do you know me?'

'Do you ask me that? Are you not Gode Silavwe and am I not the woman whose bag of beans you took without paying for it? Was it not last week when you did that at Kamwala market? Why do you pretend and ask who I am and if I know you? Do you think people haven't told me about you and your ways?'

Lines of recognition appeared on Gode's face and betrayed him to the world. But he quickly pulled himself up and assuming a stern expression, said contemptuously, 'I don't know you, woman, and I have no idea what you are talking about.'

'That's fine, but I want my bag of beans or the money for it and from no one else but you!'

'What are you talking about?'

'Don't ask me questions whose answers you know yourself. Just give me my bag of beans or the money for it. Don't trouble me, I am just a poor woman and you have already punished me enough.' She now stood with her arms akimbo, her eyes flaming with rage, poised for a physical confrontation if things came to that. The reality of her own frailty and the evident wealth and strength of the man, did not exist for her in the swirl of her anger and desperation.

Gode Silavwe sighed nervously. He thrust a hand in his trousers' side pocket and took a step backwards like a demon preparing to turn into smoke and disappear. Then ignoring her, he called out, 'Fwambo,' the name of the man with a pot-belly, and laughed a small, grotesque laugh which seemed to her crooked, devilish, stupid, repulsive.

'Honestly this town is full of mad people!' he exclaimed dismissively, and, after another scornful chuckle, he continued, 'This woman is mad. See you later. I am off, friend.'

The mixture of scorn and insolence in his attitude was as

painful as it was insulting. It revolted Nasula, and anger gave her courage.

'You will not go anywhere until you give me my bag of beans or the money for it,' she cried out. Then gripped by a sudden fit of madness, she stepped forward and threw herself at the man, grabbing both lapels of his jacket in her hands and burying her head in his belly and perfume. 'Give me my bag of beans or the money for it! Or you will have to kill me here and now!'

In the haze of her frenzy, she felt the man stagger backwards and lean against his car. He cursed in disgust. Then he hissed something that sounded obscene and struggled himself back into an upright position, his breath hot on the nape of her neck. Swiftly, his hand big and strong, he pushed against her chest with the fingers touching the lower part of her neck in a warm, moistened curve. Pushing her backwards with heavy, violent force, she felt herself fly and crash to the ground with a dull thud.

She saw redness, followed by blackness, and then silence: a momentary death and end of the world. The shock wore off and she heard the door of the car creak open. The horror of defeat passed like lightning through her brain. She pressed her lips hard together and drawing on all her will power, she tried to gather herself to her feet but collapsed to the ground again. She fought harder and just managed a kneeling position, both knees planted on the ground. Looking up in the direction of the yellow car, she saw Gode sit down on the driver's seat, though his right leg was still outside. The beast in her exploded again. She stood up, groggily, and rushed towards the car.

Gode Silavwe drew his right leg quickly into the vehicle. He closed the door and switched on the engine. Nasula grabbed the handle of the driver's door. But before she could pull it open, Gode locked it and revved the car so hard, it seemed as if he was intending to fly it instead of driving it.

126

The roaring of the engine was as intimidating as a lion's – a warning promising danger. Nasula panicked. 'Thief, thief, thief . . .' she screamed, desperately, in a possessed voice. '*Yantu mwe*, this man is a thief . . .'

People had already gathered and there was a large crowd watching everything. More were joining the crowd, asking what was happening. But not one of them was doing anything. Everyone just watched, interested only in the drama, maybe even wishing for more terrible things to happen, so that they could harvest an even more interesting story to tell to others later. Something such as the man in the car taking out a gun and shooting her.

Nasula was alone in this large and crowded world. Wildly, she began to bang on the roof of the car with her hands, crying out the word 'Thief', fumbling for what next to do.

Gode Silavwe engaged the engine. The car jerked into motion. Nasula seized hold of the handle of the rear door and pulled at it. It opened. By chance Gode had not locked it. Now the vehicle was gathering momentum. The door slipped out of her hand and banged itself closed again as she fell slightly behind.

But as she opened the door, the seat-belt on that side of the car had fallen out. Now she saw the wide black belt hanging from under the bottom edge of the rear door with the metallic hook at its end on the ground and shining brightly in the sun. She lunged forward and grabbed the belt with her left hand, letting her bag of sackcloth drop from her right shoulder. The car pulled at her with a sudden and violent force. She fell down with equal suddenness and violence, her *citenge* and tropical sandals dropping off her like beans from a dry pod that had split open after being struck against a hard stick.

There was, suddenly, a deafening noise of whistling and yelling from a terrified crowd warning the driver of the fleeing car that he was going to kill a person. One instant more, and the car would have started pulling her along. But, in the nick of time, Gode stopped the car and switched off the engine.

Nasula clung to the seat-belt more firmly, now with both hands, in a sad coil, seething and trembling, her eyes tightly closed in prayer.

'Get up,' someone standing nearby said to her after a while. 'It is over and all right, madam, you can now get up.'

She looked up and saw it was a policeman in the familiar khaki uniform, holding a gun. Relief trickled into her. She let go of the seat-belt and sat up, feeling lost and confused before the watching crowd. Beyond it the sun lay like water on the city, the concrete and glass buildings quivering in every direction.

'Here, put on your sandals,' the policeman said, dropping her torn, dusty, sweat-soiled sandals on the ground and shoving them closer to her with his booted foot. He was a young man in his early twenties, stout and broad-shouldered. His round dark eyes radiated kindness and resoluteness and it was easy to see at first glance that he was a tough but good-natured young man you could depend on in a crisis.

Still sitting, her shoulders hunched forward, she put on her tropical sandals. Meagre footwear that did nothing to hide the horniness of her dirty soles, a horniness from years of toiling barefoot in the gritty soil of her home village, a horniness which drew laughter from the more condescending and cynical portion of the crowd.

Then she rose to her feet and the policeman handed her the *citenge* and her bag of sackcloth, both of which the policeman had personally picked up. She put on the *citenge* and slung the bag over her right shoulder.

'Can you explain what the matter is?' the policeman asked her. 'You don't have to go into every detail.'

Nasula was standing to the right of the boot of the car with her back to it, facing the policeman. She looked around for Gode and saw him standing by the driver's door, his smart pinkish shirt now missing two buttons and smudged with dust and grime. These, it seemed, had come from her hair and body when she had clutched at the lapels of his jacket and plunged headfirst into him.

'He stole my bag of beans at Kamwala, last week,' she said, looking in the direction of Gode pointedly. 'I have been looking for him for many days. I found him, here, today and he is trying to run away from me.'

'Get in at the back', the policeman instructed her, pointing at Gode's car, and turning to Gode, he said, 'Let's go to Lusaka Central Police Station'.

The policeman went round the car and jumped into the car's front passenger seat next to Gode. The doors of the car banged closed in rapid succession and Gode drove off through the watching crowd of men and women transfixed with awe and amid a deafening wailing, clapping and whistling by a host of street kids.

The police station was a storeyed white building not a long drive east of Cairo Road and facing north. Entering the building you came upon a spacious hall with a high wooden Enquiries desk to the right below the first staircase leading to the floors above. When he had ushered Nasula and Gode into the hall, the policeman showed them to the only visitors' seating – a wooden platform by the eastern wall, opposite the Enquiries desk. They sat down and the policeman joined two colleagues behind the desk.

One of the two policemen at Enquiries was sitting on a waist-high stool busy writing something in a big book with thick black covers. The other was standing with his back to the counter, looking something up on a large colourful calendar that was hanging on the western wall. The two policemen were both middle-aged and older than the one who had brought Nasula and Gode to the station.

The policemen dutifully exchanged greetings, the young one saluting his older, more senior workmates. Without wasting time, the younger one busied himself looking for paper and something to write with.

A moment later, the policeman standing before the calendar turned and walked over to the counter. But when he looked in the direction of the visitors' platform, he and Gode recognised each other and exchanged smiles. The officer said something in English and Gode responded similarly. Then Gode went up to the counter and the two greeted each as warmly as good acquaintances would, shaking hands, laughing and jesting.

Gode then said something, again in English, which Nasula did not understand. She sensed something, a false explanation, more untruths, and a cold nervousness coursed through her. True to her fears, when Gode had finished talking, Nasula saw a strange glance pass between the two men; then the officer nodded and wet his lips with his tongue in a suspicious way.

After that, the officer patted the young one on the back and said something to him in English. The younger one nodded and grinned subserviently, a shade of uneasiness spreading all over his face. Then, in the vernacular, the older one told the younger one to go back to the field saying that he would handle the case that he had brought in. The former picked up his gun and as he was crossing the hall to the door, he told Nasula that his boss would deal with her case and left with an uneasy step.

The one who had been writing in the book, finished what he was writing and left the hall with the book. The other one stared at Nasula with a stern eye. Nasula's heart jumped with fear and horror.

'Madam, what evidence do you have that this is the man who

took your bag of beans?' the officer said. He was an arrogant looking man with a long face and a straight body. 'Do you have any eye witnesses?'

'Many people saw him take my bag of beans and know the truth, only they may not come forward to be my witnesses because I am just a poor woman they don't know and I am told this man is feared by many here in Lusaka.'

'I am sorry, madam. It will be difficult to help you. This man has denied ever having seen you before or ever having taken any bag of beans from anyone. I personally don't think he is the kind of man who would steal a bag of beans, and *not* from you. I think you are just mistaken.'

'I cannot understand this,' Nasula said, utterly distraught.

'You can go, madam.'

She did not move, she could not move. Cold strands she could neither see nor touch had immobilised her: they were tying her down.

'Mr Silavwe, it's all right, you can go.'

'Thank you, officer,' Gode said and started off.

After a while, the officer followed him. Nasula sensed something. She went out of the building. Standing in mute hopelessness at the verandah of the police-station building, she saw Gode Silavwe, in the driver's seat of his car, give the police officer money in several notes and then drive off.

Chapter Nine

Where there is a voice and a spirit a little more will happen . . .

She did not hear or sense, let alone see, the officer pass her, on his way back into the police station. She was beside herself. But when the turmoil inside her had subsided, she turned and looked at the Enquiries point. She saw the man standing behind the desk, reading a newspaper, the room deserted except for him.

Blood ran to her head and cheeks. Everything lost existence. She heard nothing but the pulsation in her temples and the shrill, unearthly voice in the hollows of her skull. She made up her mind and took the plunge.

Swiftly but quietly, she removed her tropical sandals, threw them into her bag of sackcloth and slipped past the Enquiries without being noticed by the officer. Reaching a corridor that ran to the east and west, she turned right towards the west. The first flight of stairs was a few steps ahead of her to the left. As she started climbing the stairs, she heard the sound of a newspaper being closed and thrown away and the shuffling of booted feet.

'Where do you think you are going?' came an officer's harsh voice. He had discovered her unauthorised passage. 'Where are you going without permission, woman?'

She did not fear and stop or answer. That she had been caught only made her more possessed with determination. She forgot about being careful in the way she moved; she carried herself along with much noise and speed. By the time the officer was at the foot of the first staircase, she was half way up the second, and moving towards the first floor.

'Come down before you get arrested!' the officer commanded authoritatively, his step sounding hurried and furious.

She started running. The noise she made as she moved increased and produced echoes in the large cavernous building. She was not sure where exactly she was going. She only ran harder and faster, her whole body steeled with stubborn determination.

A few steps near the end of the fourth staircase, towards the second floor, she tripped and fell down, badly hitting her right knee and shin against the edges of the stairs. A sharp pain tore through her leg, paralysing it for a moment. She paused briefly, gritting her teeth in pain, while listening to determine how far behind her pursuer was.

Judging from the noise coming from below, she decided the man was about to reach the first floor. She stood up and continued to climb the stairs, limping heavily and looking repeatedly over her shoulders with nervous eyes.

She reached the second floor and looked around in panic. A man in a green police uniform suddenly appeared at the extreme end of the long, high corridor of the left wing of the floor. She turned in that direction and ran as fast as the pain in her leg would allow. But the man disappeared almost as soon as he had appeared. Still she ran hard in his direction, galvanised by she knew not what instinct.

Suddenly, she rammed into someone she had not seen, who had come quietly out of one of the rooms in the corridor, and she fell down again. Without wasting time, she rose and found herself standing before a police officer who looked as if he were a man of great dignity and influence. Striking appearance. Meticulously arranged, tall, stout, dapper. He wore a green uniform and was carrying a staff in his right hand.

She cringed at the sight of him and watched her back nervously.

'What is the matter?' the officer asked. He had a pleasant voice, correct and cheerful.

'I want to see the big boss,' she said, anxiously looking about her.

'What big boss?'

'The boss of this police station; where can I find him or her?'

She looked in the direction from which she had come running. There was nobody behind her. With the help of the wooden staff he was holding, the officer motioned her to follow him into his office. She hesitated and stared at him, rooted in apprehension.

'Are you not just one of the bosses?' she asked. 'The one I want to see is the boss of everyone. The one at the topmost.'

The officer smiled a faint smile, with a wry expression on his face, making the neat, black moustache that surmounted his wide, seemingly humorous mouth, twitch just slightly.

'I cannot say that I am above everybody in this town or country,' he explained, 'but I can say that I am above everybody at this station.'

'You are the one I must see,' she said, lightened at the discovery that she was talking to the right man and that he seemed to be a good man.

The officer ushered her into his office on the northern side of that wing. It was a spacious and orderly room with white walls. When they were both inside, he closed the door and asked her to take a seat, meaning on one of the three visitors' chairs, while sitting himself down behind a large wooden table covered with green baize.

'May I know your name?' the officer said patiently after they had settled down. 'My own name is Samson Luhila. This station is under me.'

'Belita Bowa. Nasula, by my daughter's name.'

'So, feel free and explain your problem to me,' the officer said after he had scribbled down her names.

The images of her plight flooded her mind without pattern; they mingled with the sense of lenity she derived from the man before whom she sat. She became emotional and when she swallowed and tried to talk a lump came into her throat and blocked her speech. She fell into a deep, painful silence that was followed by low and muffled sounds of crying; she shook perceptibly but faintly with stifled spasms and sobs.

'Calm down,' the officer consoled her.

She felt a light drizzle of tiny drops of vapour falling over the dry tempest of rage and sorrow that lay across the landscape of her soul. Her emotions subsided. She stopped crying although tears still fell intermittently from her wet cheeks. She cleaned her face and eyes. The end of the beginning of her plight presented itself before her. She began to talk. Slowly, painfully she picked up the end of the thread and unwound it slowly before this man who was the boss of everyone at the police station. Coming to the part of the story, the events that had taken place at the police station, she lost control of herself again, and began to shake and weep as she talked.

'He, Gode, and the officer who is boss at the desk for Enquiries knew each other and it appears they have known each other for some time,' she said. 'They talked things in English, at the counter, while I sat at the bench, knowing that I can neither speak nor understand English. The boss then told the officer, who had brought us here, something in English and the young man left, telling me that his boss would deal with my case. When everybody had left, except the boss, the man who had taken my bag of beans and myself, the boss, without asking me to explain anything, said it would be difficult to do anything about my case and, just like that, he let the man go away.'

'Stop crying, don't cry.'

'Help me, I am a poor woman of no means and with no one to turn to. My daughter will not go to school after what has happened if you don't help me. She is my only one and my future. The bag of beans was my only hope of sending her to school and securing her future and mine. My only hope for my only hope!'

'When the man who stole your bag of beans went out of the building, did the officer follow him outside?'

'He did, yes he did.'

Her eyes blurred. The image of Gode Silavwe sitting in his car and passing money to the police officer who had released him came back to her. She wanted to tell Samson Luhila about the incident but something stopped her from going that far. She was afraid because she did not want to complicate things to her own disadvantage. She was not sure how Samson Luhila would take things if she told him about the incident. This was not just another policeman, but the boss of all the policemen at the police station.

'Yes, I remember very well, he followed him outside up to the car,' she simply repeated herself instead.

'What else did you see?'

'That is everything I saw.'

'You didn't see anything like the man giving the officer something?'

Nasula was tongue-tied. She fidgeted and looked down in a dither about whether or not to tell Samson Luhila the truth now that he had directly asked about the incident.

'Don't fear anything.'

'I would not want to ruin the name of any of your officers, I just want you to help me recover my bag of beans or the money for it.'

'I know that, but I also want to know the whole truth so that I can handle the case correctly and fairly.'

Silence.

'Did the man who stole your bag of beans give anything to the officer, who set him free, when he was leaving?'

Silence.

'I do understand your wanting to keep quiet about this,' Samson Luhila said, patiently. 'I know you may be afraid, but you must tell what happened. The man who stole your bag of beans gave my officer some money before he left. Is that correct?'

'He passed him several notes as he was sitting in his car, before driving away.'

'Thank you.'

Samson Luhila's face suddenly became very grave. He picked up the receiver and dialled a number. When a voice answered on the other end, he instructed the person to come and see him, without greeting the person first or saying anything in preamble. The person arrived within moments. It was the man who had dismissed Gode Silavwe. The officer, standing in the middle of the room to the left of Nasula, saluted his superior. Samson Luhila acknowledged the salutation so absently that Nasula nearly missed the act. Then he sat back in his chair and coughed lightly as if to contain himself.

'I am informed that Gode Silavwe was here again and that again he has been freed as if he had no case to answer,' Samson Luhila said very slowly and calmly. 'Is this report correct?'

'He came with her, Sir.'

'Who?'

'This woman sitting here before you, Sir.'

'Did you handle the case yourself and not the officer who arrested him?'

'I handled the case, Sir.'

Samson Luhila drew a deep breath of annoyance and, with a puckered face, leant forward and stared so hard at the other officer that you would have thought his junior was some living symbol of a shameful disease. Shaking his head in disgust, he spoke again.

'Inspector, tell me for once,' he said, 'just when are we going to finish with Gode Silavwe and the problem of innocent people who bring beans for sale at Kamwala market? Where are we going with senior officers like you?'

The inspector kept quiet, chastened. He stood at attention, but he was fright itself, a shaken stick of shame which appeared as if it might fall down and disintegrate at any moment.

'I am asking you, inspector?'

In absurd, confused, overflowing words the inspector attempted to say something about why he had taken over the case instead of leaving it to the arresting officer. But something within him disturbed his flow and he stopped talking. Then Samson Luhila told him that he was tired of his ways and that he was not going to force him to explain any further or bother to listen to him.

'Is there a vehicle at the station that is free which you can use now?' he asked.

'I am not sure, Sir,' the inspector replied, unsteadily.

Samson Luhila stood up and searched his pockets. From the side pocket of his trousers, he produced a small bunch of keys that he threw down on the table before sitting down again.

'You can use my vehicle,' he said to the inspector in a sterner but still even voice. 'Things won't end so easily for you this time. I want Gode Silavwe here and now.'

Without a word, the inspector picked up the keys from the table and walked out of the office.

A long time of waiting followed during which Samson Luhila

read and wrote things on different papers, talked on the phone, and left the office a number of times to attend to he knew better what. Nasula sat in her chair doing nothing but furtively watching the police officer in action. Her mind was blank.

She did not know what to think or expect. At last, the knock came, the door opened and the inspector entered the office accompanied by Gode Silavwe, the latter as usual suited and wearing a tie. He had changed into a khaki green suit and white, striped shirt. Smart. Sharply scented perfume.

Nasula's heart leapt. She sat herself properly and gazed at Samson Luhila in curious anticipation. The latter stopped writing and sat back with the confidence of a stout-hearted man. The inspector saluted his superior with a heavy thumping of his feet and brisk, powerful movements of his arms. You could see that nothing was more prominent in his heart than a terrified desire to pacify his boss. But ignoring the inspector's flamboyant display of dutifulness and without welcoming either of the two or showing them seats, Samson Luhila commanded Gode Silavwe to listen to him carefully.

'I don't expect you to make this case more complicated for yourself than it is already,' he said firmly, 'I expect you to be honest and straightforward with yourself. Do you recognise this woman?'

Gode Silavwe coughed and shifted, evidently confused and shaken.

'Look at her properly before you answer me,' advised Samson Luhila. 'Do you recognise her or not?'

'I have recognised her.'

'Did you take her bag of beans?'

'I did.'

The shock of relief descended upon Nasula like a lightning bolt. Sudden, swift, bright. A shower of the rain of light and hope crossed the parched and dusty grounds of her dejection and despair. She wiped her mouth with her hand and cupped her chin in her palm, shaking her head lightly in disbelief. Was this Gode Silavwe? Was this the very man who had stolen her bag of beans accepting his offence in broad daylight?

'Is the bag still there?'

'I have used it.'

'Did you pay for it?'

'I was going to pay for it.'

'I won't ask you any more questions now,' Samson Luhila said with a note of finality. He was visibly irritated. 'We shall deal with the rest later. This woman comes from very far away and has been sleeping at the inter-city bus terminus for a week without eating or washing because of what you did to her. She has been looking for you all this time. She is stranded. The bag of beans you took from her was her only hope of money for her food, her travel back to the village and for sending her only daughter to school when it opens this coming Monday. I want you to give her the money for her bag of beans now so that she can go back to her home.'

'I only have fifty thousand *kwacha* just here,' Gode Silavwe said, meekly, dipping his hand into first this pocket and then that.

'A bag of beans at Kamwala is going for how much at this time of the year?'

'One hundred . . .'

'One hundred and twenty thousand *kwacha*,' Nasula quickly answered, afraid Gode Silavwe might lie to the officer.

'I thought it was one hundred and fifty thousand,' Samson Luhila said.

'That is the price for the *kabulangeti* one,' Gode Silavwe corrected; 'hers was the yellow and white mixed type.'

'You give her one hundred and fifty thousand *kwacha*,' Samson Luhila commanded. 'You have troubled her a lot.

Regard the way she is looking. Does it please you to see a mother looking like this?'

'I'll give her one hundred and fifty thousand *kwacha* as you have suggested, Sir.'

Samson Luhila ignored his acquiescence and turned to the inspector in a no less dismissive way.

'John, go with him,' he said. 'Let him raise one hundred and fifty thousand *kwacha* and bring it here without fail. I expect you to be back in an hour's time. This woman is tired and hungry.'

'Instruction taken, Sir,' the inspector said and saluted in the same exuberant way meant to pacify his boss. Then he asked Gode Silavwe to follow him in such an impersonal manner that you would have thought the other was a total stranger, almost an enemy.

Not a very long time passed. The inspector and Gode Silavwe returned. The inspector saluted and Samson Luhila asked Gode Silavwe if he had come with the money he had ordered him to bring with him. Gode Silavwe said he had brought the money and fished out a bunch of folded green notes from one of the inside pockets of his jacket.

'Give it to her,' Samson Luhila ordered.

Gode Silavwe stepped forward and handed Nasula the money. Nasula shifted in her chair, overwhelmed.

'Count it and make sure it is not a *kwacha* less,' Samson Luhila told her.

Nasula left the chair she had been sitting on and knelt down with both her knees planted on the floor, and she lined the ten thousand *kwacha* notes Gode Silavwe had given her on the floor and counted them. The notes were fifteen.

'How much has it come to?' Samson Luhila asked her when she had finished counting.

'One fifty.'

141

'Keep it safely.'

Nasula gathered the money from the floor, her heart strings tender with satisfaction and vibrating to a silent tune about struggle and the long arm of the spirit. One hundred and fifty thousand *kwacha* instead of one hundred and twenty thousand *kwacha*? Suffering woman? *Iye kalanda we!*

As Nasula began to undo the knot at the end of her *citenge* where she kept the money, Samson Luhila turned to the inspector and began issuing fresh instructions. His voice had mellowed but he still sounded annoyed with the inspector and Gode Silavwe.

'Take this man to the Criminal Investigation Department,' he said. 'Leave him there for the constable who arrested him to come and handle the paperwork. Tell whoever is there that my instructions are that after this has been done and a docket opened, he must be locked up. You yourself should return here quickly, so that you can write a statement from this woman, in my presence, before she goes.'

When he returned from leaving Gode Silavwe at the CID, the inspector pulled up one of the visitors' chairs and sat down on it next to Nasula, pen and paper in hand. As politely and as diligently as he was able in an endeavour to impress his boss, he asked for and wrote down Nasula's particulars: her full name, tribe, village, chief, district, province, age, and so on.

Then he settled down to writing out the details of the case: what had transpired from the time she had arrived in Lusaka to that very moment, including the part involving Gode Silavwe giving several *kwacha* bills to the inspector.

Nasula had wanted to leave out that part, but Samson Luhila who had been following her narration attentively as he had worked on his own papers, urged her to include the detail as she had earlier disclosed it to him. As he wrote, the inspector's broad lips became a frozen grimace of fear and his look wavered. It must have been a terrible ordeal for him. Nasula could not help but dart anxious glances at the man as he wrote down his own role in the story of her plight.

When everything was complete, the inspector read it through and interpreted what he had written down to her from the English.

'Do you agree to having said everything I have written and read to you?' he then asked her. 'Or you have some objections?'

'Everything is as I have told you.'

'Is there anything else you would like to add to what I have already written down?'

'No.'

'Are you going to sign or use your thumb?'

'I will use my thumb.'

The inspector went out of the office and brought an ink-pad and Nasula committed her thumb to her statement.

'Let me have the papers,' Samson Luhila demanded as soon as Nasula and the inspector were through. The inspector passed him the two papers, each of which the policeman had filled out on both sides. Samson Luhila pinned the two papers together and put them aside. He next picked from his table three papers with both printed and handwritten words, that had been pinned together. He handed these papers to the inspector.

'Read what's there carefully,' he said as gravely as a medicine man about to disempower a witch. 'I have suspended you, while the charges against you are investigated, and you are on suspension starting from now.'

The inspector, speechless, froze into a brittle stillness. His big, black, flashing eyes became distant in that very instance, unblinking, as in death. In the spur of the moment, Nasula could not help but feel sorry for him. Samson Luhila looked at her, and sighed as though he had only just discovered her presence in his office and realised that he shouldn't have said what he had just said to his officer in her presence. He told her that it was all over and she could go.

Nasula rose pushing the chair behind her to create a little space, her heart quivering. She was astounded by the power and heart of the man, and the world his office had opened up to her.

'Thank you very much,' she said to him. 'You have saved me and my daughter. We are poor people with nowhere to clap a hand. May the gods and spirits continue lighting the path for you in your work and wherever you go.'

'We are here for you. Go well.'

'Remain well.'

With these words, a sweet warmth flooding her, she bowed to Samson Luhila, and bringing her hands together reverently, she passed the frozen figure of the inspector and walked out of the office into the silence and stillness of the corridor, limping only slightly.

The woman was elated. She walked with a sure step and a buoyant heart. She felt strong and refreshed in spite of her tired, dirty, smelly, aching body with hunger eating at the walls of her stomach, and the thirst that pulled at her mouth. The pain in her knee and leg was still there, but it did not bother her. It was as if it had ceased to exist.

Outside, the sun had descended considerably, but it was still quite a way from the horizon. She put on her tropical sandals and went to Kamwala shopping centre. There she started buying the things her daughter had told her were needed for school.

She bought new things only. Nothing second-hand. She was happy for her daughter. For the first time in a long time, Sula would own new things straight from a shop. The first thing she bought was the girl's travelling bag, a dark blue suitcase like a bag with wheels. In it she put what other things she bought.

It was getting late. The shops were about to close. There was only one thing left remaining for her to buy. It was the thing she had planned to buy last because of its bulkiness and the problem it would give her carrying it. She entered the shop where she had seen the cheapest item.

'Give me that,' she told a male shop attendant, leaning over the counter and pointing at a green cotton mattress.

The shop attendant, a small round man with a beard, fetched a ladder and brought down the mattress from the top of a roof-high shelf. She paid for the mattress. The shop attendant folded it into a roll and tied it firmly with sisal rope and placing it on the counter, told her she could take it. She lifted the mattress on to her head. Balancing the mattress with the help of her left hand, she lifted the travelling bag with her right hand and started towards the door. She had shifted her bag of sackcloth to her left shoulder.

She was standing at the doorway of the shop when someone passing in front of it, called out her name in a voice full of shock and amazement. It was Nalukwi.

'Nasula, is it you that my eyes are seeing?' marvelled Nalukwi, staring at her in disbelief.

The younger woman came out of the shop and stood to one side of the door. She put the travelling bag down against the wall, then brought the mattress down from her head and placed it carefully beside the travelling bag.

'*Ala!*' exclaimed Nalukwi, horror flooding her eyes at the sight of Nasula. 'You did not go to the village? Hmm, Nasula, the way you look. What has been happening to you?'

'It is a story that is long, Nalukwi, the story of everything that has happened since I left your home,' Nasula said and looked at the mattress and the blue travelling bag cordially as if the property were a pair of twins she had just delivered after an excruciating labour. 'But everything is all right now. I found the man and got the money from him. I have just been buying things for the school-going one.'

'You found the man who stole your bag of beans?'

'I found the man.'

'Gods, spirits! What can I say, Nasula of ours? I thought you were in the village by now. The boy I sent to see you off then must have lied to me. He told me he left you at the station after he had already bought the bus ticket for you.'

'It was not a lie he told you. He bought the ticket for me. I even got on the bus. But before we reached Kabwe, something told me to come back. I got out of the bus when it stopped at a road-block. The conductor took a share of the money I had paid for the fare and gave me back the rest.'

'And you returned?'

'I jumped on a minibus and came back. I started looking for the man and I managed to catch him today itself.'

'What suffering you must have gone through. I can see this for you have become so thin and dirty, Nasula of ours. And why couldn't you come home?'

'How was I going to find my way?'

'Do I have words?' Nalukwi said and clapped her hands. 'Come, we shall talk some more later. Now, let us go home and then you can wash and eat something. Have you bought yourself something different to wear?'

'No.'

'Do you have something like ten thousand *kwacha* which you can spare for yourself?'

'Ten thousand *kwacha*? I think I have.'

'Come, there are cheap second-hand dresses and shoes at the market. We can get something for you to change into after you have washed.'

Nalukwi lifted the travelling bag and Nasula scooped up the mattress and put it on her head. They crossed the road in front of the line of shops to the west of Kamwala market. They went to the section for *salaula* and there Nasula bought herself a flowered dress of many colours and a pair of blue canvas shoes. Then they proceeded to the town centre and boarded a minibus to Mandevu shanty compound.

The house in which Nalukwi and her family lived was a three-roomed ramshackle with brick walls and a roof of miscellaneous scrap-metal. The yard around the house was a meagre piece of bare greyish ground shorn of its topsoil. The only other structures there were a brick and scrap-metal latrine and an elephant grass bath fence. The home was a metaphor of poverty. But it felt good being there. It was refreshing to be in a home away from the wilderness and insecurity of the streets and the bus station.

The woman bathed and changed into her newly acquired second-hand dress and shoes. Then she ate *nshima* with boiled *kapenta* and vegetables and drank a lot of water. After she had eaten, she sat down on a reed mat outside the house and relaxed. Washed, fully fed and in clean clothes, she felt like a newly born baby; and clothed in the aura of her victory and success, she looked forward to her journey back to the village, with perfect hope. She started dozing and slept on the reed mat.

Later in the evening after the family had eaten supper, Nalukwi and her husband, a soft-spoken man with a big body, came and joined her and she told them the story of her search for Gode Silavwe.

In the morning, the following day, Nalukwi escorted her to the inter-city bus terminus and saw her off on a bus to Mpulungu. A white bus with a blue line on its sides. A good new bus, a bus of the nineties.

The journey started in earnest and with a sense of great joy. The woman with every speck of her being was part of the crowd and part of the activity on the bus – eating, chatting, jesting, exchanging food, passing valuables and helping with change. There was life in the bus and she was part of that life.

The sun went down in the west and it was night. A thick darkness fell upon the world. The bus opened its eyes and bathed the road before it with sharp yellow light. In the cool empty silence of the night the bus acquired a fresh breath of life. It roared and moved onward with strength and zeal, like a lion running after a tiring gazelle.

The driver of the bus, to vary the monotony of the rumba that he had been playing on the music system, and as if according to God's plan, fed his music machine with a tape containing vernacular church songs. The passengers began to sing along and filled the bus with the hearty Christian music of their voices. 'When I was born,' they sang, 'I thought there was happiness here on earth, dear friends. When I grew up I knew only of the life of hardship and sorrow. Dear friends, today, let me cry.'

In another song, they warned the non-believer to be careful and not take the world for granted. The creator alone, they said, was light and truth. The Almighty God was a powerful God, Jesus Christ His Son would come. Yes, the Messiah would return. Jesus Christ would surely come back to this earth.

Nasula, not being a woman of the church, did not know the songs. But they sounded delicious to her heart, caressing her spirit with a power beyond tenderness. Nasula found herself swimming in their warmth and transported into another world. She began to sing with the rest of the passengers. And the bus roared along devouring the distance.

The bus stopped at Senga Hill, her destination, towards midnight. Mattress on her head and travelling bag in hand and the bag of sackcloth hung over her left shoulder, Nasula braved the night and set out on the long walk to Swelini as soon as she had alighted from the bus. As the sun was beginning to descend the sky, the following day, she entered the yard of her home and saw Sula, her daughter, standing in the doorway of their hut.

She stopped walking, in the middle of the yard, and gazed at the slender, beautiful figure of her daughter, her heart throbbing, and tears welling up in her eyes.

The daughter saw her and, after a moment of stillness, started running towards her. Nasula threw down the bags and mattress and ran to meet the girl, and daughter and mother met and embraced.

Words were hard to come between them. But they picked up the thread and communicated their fears, hopes, sadnesses and joys. The mother gave the daughter what she had bought for her. Everything fitted the daughter so well she was born with it on her body. Sula danced and sang. The mother clapped and smiled happily for her. Sula brought out the paper on which her new school had listed what each student needed to take with her. Mother and daughter went through the list together, checking everything the mother had brought, her daughter ticking off each item. Everything was there. Nasula had not left out anything.

At first cockcrow the following morning, Nasula escorted Sula to Senga Hill. Late in the afternoon, Sula jumped on a bus for her journey to Kasama for St Theresa Secondary School. As the bus started moving, mother and daughter waved emotionally at each other and wept. When the bus had disappeared, Nasula sighed with relief and began her journey back to Swelini.

Glossary

The language used in the text is Mambwe.

Abaleya, abaleya, abaleya . . . *Abali* busy, *abali* busy, *abali* busy . . . *Washala, abaleya!*	Bemba and English words of encouragement meant to urge the passengers to hurry along
ala	interjection meaning 'Really!' or 'Surely!' depending on the context
Ata!	an impatient, contemptuous exclamation
cisense	a type of small fish not dissimilar to a sardine
citenge	a length of material which may be used as a dress, skirt, wrapper for a baby, a covering, or mat
dambo	wetland
icisongole	a hard-shelled tropical wild fruit
iciyenga	a game played by girls which is similar to jacks or *nhodo*: a stone is thrown in the air, and before it lands other stones must be gathered into the hand
iye	exclamation
Iye kalanda we!	exclamation: in the context meaning something like, 'Oh poor one!'
Iye mwe!	exclamation
kabulangeti	a type of bean
kakonko	a type of music
kapenta	small fresh-water fish resembling a sardine, often salted and dried

kaponda	a type of local tobacco
kwacha	unit of Zambian currency
mama	respectful term for woman of middle years
Mambwe	Zambian tribe and language found in the extreme north of Zambia near the Tanzanian border
musanze	elephant grass
namukokolo	the north star
ngwee	smallest unit of Zambian currency
nshima	stiff porridge
Owe!	interjection expressing surprise
punku	a diarrhoeal disease
pupwe	a wild vegetable with a texture like okra when cooked
salaula	second-hand clothes or shoes
yantu mwe	you people
yantu yakwe Leza!	exclamation: God's people!
Zezulu	a man or woman belonging to the Goregore tribe